HIS LONELY REIGN

DARK HEART SERIES BOOK ONE

LILLITH CARRIE

First paperback edition April 2023

ISBN 979-8-89034-872-2

Published by Lillith Carrie Publishing

www.lillithcarriepublishing.com

To those who seek the darkness to find the one they love...
Never be afraid of the adventure. Even through the darkest of
nights we find the light.
Love Always,
Lillith Carrie

MEETING MR. SOLVMANE

YOU CAN DO THIS... I mentally told myself. *No distractions.*

Gazing up at the dark, looming building in front of me, I admired the white and black letters: Solv Logistics. The building was no different from any other skyscraper in New York City, but somehow it seemed more intimidating—more menacing.

Like a giant towering over the ant-like figures walking the sidewalks, it cast shadows across the city with no care in the world other than to stand out amongst the sky. The sleek black walls were made up of windows that seemed to ward off the sunlight rather than reflect it. My anxiety was currently through the roof, taking a deep breath though, I pressed forward in my Mary Jane pumps to the glass double doors that waited for me ahead.

Solv Logistics was a reputable company headquartered in NYC for decades. They specialized in transportation of anything, and had been globally known for helping in humanitarian situations. So when new intel came into my father's company, Elite Humanity, there was more under the surface, well, it took everyone by surprise. I drew the short end of the stick, forced to investigate what was actually going on behind the high-rise walls of regalia.

When I stepped inside the building, I was taken back by how beautiful it was. Gazing around at the dark velvet seating, and the coffee center brewing the most delicious aromas, I realized I wasn't in Kansas anymore. The designers had outdone themselves, and though the black, gold, and white toned decor were simple, it really gave way to how serious they took themselves.

Or how much this company prided itself on being the best in its industry.

"Damn," I breathed out softly.

"Miss, did you need something?" The voice of a man pulled me back to the present. I turned my attention to the main reception area and found a huge, burly looking security guard with dark eyes and an annoyed expression.

At least he's human.

"Yes, I actually have an interview this morning."

Raising a brow, his eyes drifted up and down my attire with curiosity. "The secretary position... yes. Mr. Grey told me a young woman would be coming. What's your name?"

"Sydney," I replied, trying to keep my composure. Something about this man just seemed off, and the way he was staring at me creeped me out.

"Does Sydney have a last name?" he asked flatly.

Nodding, I cleared my throat. "Yeah...sorry. It's Adams."

Typing away at the computer, he picked up a card and ran it through a card reader before holding it out to me. When I went to take it, he held onto it and stared at me just a bit longer. "You look familiar. Do I know you from somewhere?"

Shit. Shit. Shit.

"No," I replied, shaking my head slowly. "I'm new around here so I doubt it. I just moved here from California."

"California? It says on the paperwork you're from Iowa."

I had almost forgotten that little bit of information. I did put that I was from Iowa and, thinking quickly, I smiled at him. "Yep, that's where I was born. I went to school out west and lived there for a few years. That is until I landed the chance at moving to the Big Apple."

The security guard seemed hesitant for a moment before reluctantly releasing the card. "Very well. Go straight through this checkpoint and scan your card. Then take the elevator up to your floor. You only have access to the fourteenth floor."

I didn't bother to wait around to have him question me further. Bidding him a thank you and goodbye, I quickly made my way past the checkpoint scanner and straight towards the elevators, where a few others waited patiently to enter.

All my years of training I hadn't been scared of much, but today I couldn't shake this dreadful feeling in my stomach, I was taking on more than I could handle. Wiping my sweaty palms on my skirt, my eyes stared at the numbers above the elevator, watching them count down until the doors had finally opened.

"After you," a woman said, causing me to snap my gaze towards my left, coming face to face with the true form of Succubus. Her curved horns shimmered blue as the scaled markings on the side of her face contrasted with her golden green eyes. I had never seen a succubus in person before, and I tried my best not to stare, but damn it—I couldn't help it.

"Are you okay, dear?" she asked, snapping me out of my daze with a furrowed brow of confusion. "Do you need help?"

"Oh, I'm sorry," I replied, shaking my head. "My mind is all over the place. I have my first interview today with the CEO, and I will admit I'm really nervous."

It wasn't entirely a lie, but I was trying to save face, so this woman didn't notice I knew she wasn't human. After a moment, her face softened as she nodded in what seemed to be understanding. "Oh, I get it. Don't worry yourself, sweetie. He isn't that bad at all."

"Thank you, I hope he likes me. I really want this job."

The conversation died as we piled into the elevator. Almost half of the people in the elevator with me were supernatural. Their glamor might have fooled normal humans, but not me. My great-great-grandfather had fixed that minor problem with some chemistry and a quick pinch of a needle long ago. All of us were given what we called the X-vac—a shot that allowed us to see these monsters for what they truly were.

Because of that, I had a new nifty gift that allowed me to do my job a lot better.

Still, I couldn't help but shiver as I kept my eyes forward. The human beside me was completely oblivious, flicking through a file of papers as she muttered to herself. I wish I could tell her to run. To leave the company and never come back, but that would just give me away. I had to act normal.

Besides, New York City was supposed to be a neutral territory. I wasn't allowed to do anything, even if I wanted to.

It seemed like every floor we hit, the elevator stopped and the doors would open, letting people off until finally, I was the only one remaining. The doors swished open, revealing a smaller version of the lobby downstairs, minus the coffee, which I wished I had gotten before I'd come up.

More velvet chairs surrounded a sleek couch set to my right. The company's name hung on the wall to my left in gold, bright against the black background. Ahead of me was a secretary's desk, also black, but the only part of her I could see was the top of her head.

"Excuse me?" I said clearly, forcing myself to walk up to that desk, another fake smile plastered on my face as I tried to seem as natural as possible.

The woman's head snapped up, human eyes meeting mine, giving me an internal sigh of relief.

"Take a seat. Mr. Grey will be with you in a moment."

Taken aback by the woman's brash response, I thanked her again before doing just that. Perched at the end of the couch, I glance around. Most of the offices around where I was sitting had their doors closed, and though I couldn't hear them talking on their phones, I was able to see them through the blinds in their windows.

Creatures of all sizes, and species; from Fae to Harpies, Succubus to Shifters, even a Nymph in the distance pouring coffee in what seemed to be a break room carried on as if everything was normal. Then again, I suppose for those here it was.

I just couldn't believe the amount of humans working alongside shifters, who had absolutely no clue what kind of danger they were in. Something my father would be eager to know once I was done with this interview.

Not that I was looking forward to that conversation. The man may have been my father, but he wasn't a very likable person and his confidence in me was minimal. I was only here because it was what my grandfather wanted. Nothing more, nothing less.

"Ms. Adams?" a voice called out as the most gorgeous man I had ever seen stepped through the glass doors around the corner.

He was tall and slim, his tailored, three-piece suit clearly more expensive than the rent on my downtown apartment. Even the rigid way he stood made him appear to have definitely come from the upper class. I doubted that the faint lines carved into the skin around his eyes and lips were because the man smiled a lot.

On top of his freakishly gorgeous looks, it only took a moment for me to realize he was a fucking vampire.

No wonder you're gorgeous. You're a blood-sucking killer.

Pulling myself together, I jumped to my feet holding out my hand. "Hello, I'm Sydney Adams."

He eyed me as if I were the monster. The tips of his fangs peeked out beneath his upper lip as they formed a sneer. Dragging my eyes up, I hoped he hadn't noticed my slip-up when I was gawking at his teeth, but I couldn't help it. I'd never actually shook the hand of a vampire before. I'd only killed one.

"You can follow me," he replied flatly, ignoring my offer of a handshake as he quickly turned around and began walking back the way he had come.

Aren't you a ray of fucking sunshine... I muttered to myself as I followed him down a long hallway that wrapped around the building, with offices lined up on either side. People scurried between them, doors opening and closing, stacks of papers being carried or rolled out on trolleys. I weaved through the slight crowd, trying to follow who I assumed was Mr. Grey.

"This floor is for inventory management and data collection," Mr. Grey explained, speed-walking down the hallway. Well, I guess it was a normal speed for him—speed-walking for me. "You'll be Mr. Solvmane's personal assistant, so you'll need to know what each floor and department does and the usual ins and outs."

"Oh." Was this an interview or fucking orientation? And I knew absolutely nothing about what a logistics company actually did. Maybe my cover as a new-to-town college graduate wasn't well thought out. "Alright."

"Your resume did say you were a fast learner." Mr. Grey glanced over his shoulder at me with his eyes narrowed.

"I am," I reassured him, perking up. My smile didn't seem to affect him at all. Instead, he curled his lip with a look of disgust as he slid his eyes away from me and pushed open another door. I stopped short when I realized we were right back in the lobby. Mr. Grey was unfazed, already pressing the button for the elevators as if he couldn't wait for all of this to be over, and when they opened, I had to rush to jump in next to him, otherwise I was certain he would have left me behind.

It was like that for the next thirty minutes as we went to each floor, speed-walking around the halls as he quickly explained what each department did. I tried to keep up. I really did. By the end of this tour, my mind was just as exhausted as my feet.

And there was no way I remembered half of what he told me.

So much for just a simple interview.

"And that's about it." Mr. Grey stepped out of the elevator—hopefully for the last time. We had gone all the way up to the last floor and it took a moment for me to realize this must have been the big man's office. I could see out the windows across the small lobby, overlooking Manhattan. It was a gorgeous view, but unfortunately, Mr. Grey didn't give me long to admire it before he was calling my name again.

"Ms. Adams?" Mr. Grey's slender eyebrow rose as he gave me a disdainful look.

"Coming." Ducking my head, I hurried after him, feet protesting the entire way. I mean, if I knew I was going to walk this much just for an interview, I wouldn't have worn platforms. Instead, I would have come more relaxed and with a notebook to take notes so I could actually remember everything he was telling me.

There was no doubt if I wandered off on my own that I would get lost. I needed a map to get through this damn place.

"And this will be your desk," Mr. Grey said, stopping just beside the office door. "Do you think you can manage to remember all this or do you need me to make you notes?"

"You have notes—"

He scoffed at my comment, and I quickly realized he was being sarcastic. Why in the hell would he want to make me notes? "I've got it. I don't need notes... it's all stored away in my head."

Curling his lip again, he rolled his eyes. "Yes, I suppose we will see how true that really is, won't we?"

Fucking dick.

My eyes swept over the desk he had gestured to moments before. There was nothing special about it. Just a desktop computer, a laptop, a few pens, a notepad and a black, stocky swivel chair.

"Mr. Grey."

I nearly jumped out of my skin as I whipped to the left. The door of the office was open and a man I didn't recognize stood just inside the doorway staring at me. He was handsome—no, scratch that—the man was downright sinful. He towered over me, broad shoulders barely contained by his jacket or blue suit. His black hair was slicked back and shaved on the sides. The tips of black ink upon his skin barely poked out beneath his collar.

When my eyes caught the silvery gray of his, I thought my heart stopped.

Not just because of his looks, but because of what he was.

It took everything in me not to recoil as he studied me. It took everything not to run right out those damn doors. My dad had said there might be a supernatural running the company here. That it would lead us to what we were actually looking for—whatever that was.

However, he said nothing about the CEO being a Lycan.

THE MYSTERIOUS MISS ADAMS

NOAH

~Half-hour Before~

The minute I picked up the phone, I knew I wasn't going to be happy.

"Boss?"

"What is it, Ace?" I sighed, hand lifting to run my fingers through my hair before I remembered I had an important investment meeting later, and if I messed up my hair, Janice, my public relations manager, would kill me. She was a harpy with a bad attitude when personal appearances were made to be anything but perfect.

"We've got an issue," he replied. Gritting my teeth in response, I dropped my hand back to the desk, slowly curling it into a fist.

"I figured since you were calling," I said with a heavy breath. "What now?"

"There's been another attack—"

Of course there fucking was.

Years I spent working to get my empire on top to ensure I could set a good example for other supernaturals in the world, and yet no matter how good things got... I constantly hit snags at every turn. Lately, those snags were in the forms of supernatural killings.

Killings that left no answers to the questions constantly being thrown my way.

Which was another reason why my phone never stopped ringing off the hook. Letting out a low groan, I ran my hand over my face.

Trying to remain calm, I pulled myself together, knowing my men were already hesitant towards me when it came to delivering bad news. The last time I had been told less-than-stellar news was when my wife had been killed, and that news caused me to almost kill one of my guards.

It wasn't their fault the incident had happened, but I wasn't an easy man to talk to when it came to death. Death and I weren't on the same page, so it seemed. Yet, if he came now—after losing her... I'd probably welcome him like an old friend. "Where?"

"Subway. 110th street."

Leaning back in my chair, I stared at the ceiling trying to collect my thoughts. "Start from the beginning. What happened?"

"Two vampires were rounded up. Which doesn't make any sense. New York City is neutral territory. Everybody knows this. Not that it stopped the humans from accusing them."

"What are the charges?" I asked, completely ignoring his rambling.

"Elite Humanity claimed they attacked a human."

"And did they?"

"I—"

"Did they attack a human?" I asked again.

"I'm not sure just yet."

"Then find out and get back to me," I snapped and hung up before I could hear more.

This was the same shit that had been happening for weeks, and though I wanted to believe the supernaturals weren't actually lashing out at humans, I had begun to question it all. There was no way Elite Humanity would be this stupid to cause issues.

It just didn't make sense.

If these vamps really did attack a human, Elite Humanity had every right to put them down. That was the way things were. We followed the rules, and no one got hurt. That was simple and clear; don't attack the humans. Don't cause problems. But Elite Humanity was never one to follow rules—even their own.

Leaning forward, my elbows pressed into the wood. My fingers laced together, the knuckles turning white. I'm not sure what anyone expected me to do about any of this—especially if the supernaturals were as guilty as Elite Humanity kept claiming. Without proof of their innocence, there was no way to protect them.

Fuck, why does this shit have to be so difficult all the time?

Footsteps coming down the hall caught my attention, pulling me from my thoughts. I could hear Mr. Grey's voice well enough, though it wasn't his steps I heard. Vampires were too quiet for even my senses to catch. The scent of a human woman drifted into my office, powerful and distracting. Freezing, I listened as they came closer.

"And this will be your desk." Mr. Grey's voice was silky and smooth but lifeless. There was never any emotion to his words, which I rather liked. With him, everything was concise and to the point.

His shadow fell across the door of my office, with a smaller one moving toward the secretary's desk just beside him. Her words were slightly muffled as I listened to what sounded like a sarcastic comment from him, followed by nervous female laughter. Grey wasn't funny at all... in fact, most called him an assshole, so the laughter was concerning. Glancing at my calendar on the computer screen, I noticed the small appointment Grey had set up earlier.

New Secretary Interview.

Well, crap.

Absolutely perfect. Might as well check out what he had brought me.

Standing to my feet I straightened my suit jacket and smoothed back my hair. The stress of Ace's call fell away, leaving nothing but cold indifference as I headed toward my office door. Stepping out, I saw Grey right away. He studied the human girl with narrowed eyes filled with distaste. The woman, I didn't see much of at first. Her dark red hair fell over her face, hiding it from view as she surveyed her desk. Her curves were just barely contained in a black pencil skirt and white blouse.

"Mr. Grey."

The woman jumped slightly, whipping around to face me as I leaned against the office door, watching her reaction. Her emerald eyes swept over me, widening before flicking up to meet mine. Something I couldn't quite place passed over her face; surprise, maybe fear?

I could certainly smell a multitude of emotions rolling off her in waves. A mixture of jasmine and roses swept through me like a garden I had once visited with my mother when I was younger. As her scent hit me again, like a sucker punch to the gut, I straightened, trying to ignore it. Whatever that was, I had no intention of letting it get to me.

"Is this the woman you're interviewing to be my secretary?" I asked casually, my eyes never leaving her face.

"Yes," Mr. Grey replied. I could hear the 'but' in his voice, but didn't press the issue.

Instead, I stepped closer, glancing down at her small petite frame. I towered over her by a good few inches. She was almost pixie-like, around—what, five foot four? Despite the luscious thickness to her hips and her chest, I could break her easily enough. Her green eyes narrowed, almost as if she could hear my thoughts.

Yet, she said nothing.

"This isn't an easy job," I murmured, watching as the hair along her arms rose at the sound of my voice. "You'll need to be able to track the reports and files from each of the different departments, schedule meetings, collect the quarterlies from each department head, among...other things."

Her throat bobbed slightly at that last part. I hadn't meant for it to come out as sultry as it had. She was beautiful—for a human. Eyes as rich as emeralds, lips as red as blood. Her porcelain skin worked well with the soft burgundy of her natural red hair. And that body...Clearing my throat, I forced myself to turn away.

Mr. Grey caught my eye. "Well?"

"If you believe she can handle the work, then let's give it a try," I replied, words dripping with indifference. It didn't really matter to me whether or not she could keep up. There were always more secretaries. More humans. Though the others had never intrigued me as much as this one did.

Grey wrinkled his nose slightly, a movement too quick for the woman to catch. But I did.

"Then that's settled," I said quickly. "Get her the paperwork."

Surprise flashed across Grey's eyes. "Sir?"

I don't know what made me do it. Maybe it was her scent that had my mind blanking. Or maybe I was just too damn tired to deal with another issue on top of everything else. It really shouldn't have been this hard to find a replacement secretary. I wasn't exactly easy to please, so maybe it was. Regardless, for some odd reason I wanted her around.

"Paperwork," I said again, slower this time. A hint of a warning lined my tone. "Unless there's an issue I don't know about?" With one eyebrow raised, I waited for his reply.

"None, sir." Grey's shoulders stiffened, which was a feat unto itself, considering vamps were always stiff.

"Excellent." I glanced over my shoulder at the woman who resembled more of an owl than a human at this point. "And you are...?"

She swallowed again, drawing my gaze to her throat. "Sydney."

"Sydney, what?"

"Adams." The word sounded unfamiliar on her tongue.

"Grey, please take Ms. Adams to sign the paperwork and get her set up." I didn't wait for his answer. I didn't look at her again, either. The scent of jasmine and roses filled my nose, making my head light. I needed to get out of there.

I needed her to get her away from me, at least until I could clear my head.

My office door swished shut, the lock clicking in place. I stood there for a few minutes, hand wrapped so tightly around the handle, the metal nearly bent beneath it. There was a slight hesitation from Grey before he briskly ordered Sydney to follow him once again. Even though the door was closed, I couldn't get her beautiful green eyes out of my head.

Sydney.

She seemed young and sweet enough. However, I was hesitant on whether she would be able to do the job I needed her to do. Not to mention she was human, which meant I had to be careful in the office—but that wasn't anything new. I'd purposely hired humans to work in my company to show Elite Humanity that I could play nice, that all of us could play nice. So far, it's run smoother than butter. They were treated well. Paid well.

Sydney would be no different.

But it felt different. Even as I listened to the elevator doors shut down the hall, I could still smell her. Her presence lingered in the hall, drifting in through the cracks of the door. Closing my eyes, I took another deep breath. It had been a long time since a woman had gotten me bent out of shape, for a woman to make my beast stand on edge. Pushing away from the door, I stalked back towards my desk, forcing myself to sit down.

"Shit," I huffed out to myself. I needed a drink, but unfortunately polished off the rest of my sanity over the last few days dealing with other shit.

Taking a moment, I let my mind clear and as soon as I did, guilt ripped through me. My eyes caught on the framed photo on my desk, the only personal item I allowed in my office. In it, a woman smiled back, looking so wild. Carefree. Her dark hair whipped back from her face, frozen in time as she sat on the beach. Her tanned skin glowed, her silver eyes bright.

My mate.

Roya had been my whole world. My everything. We'd been mates for so long, surviving together, building together. Until Elite Humanity took it all away. Took her away.

My claws snapped out, raking across my desk. Elite Humanity was the bane of our existence. Our overlords that no one could defy. They'd had centuries to perfect their killings, their plans. They outnumbered us in more ways than one. And I knew, better than anyone, not to mess with the fire lest I wanted it all to burn.

Jasmine and roses mixed in the air, taunting me. Maybe it had been a mistake to hire the woman. There was something off about her... something that bothered me, though I couldn't pinpoint why. I'd hired her without thinking. As if I'd been possessed by something I couldn't explain.

I was back on my feet before I realized what I was doing. I just knew I had to get out of here before whatever spell that woman had me under tore me apart. The memories, the feelings of loss, left me completely useless. Grabbing my things, I tucked my phone into the suit jacket and slipped out the door. Hoping to keep out of view, but at the same time knowing that I wouldn't be able to escape her.

Especially since the scent of her followed me all the way to my car.

And would more than likely follow me home.

SWEET FAMILY REUNIONS

SYDNEY

As soon as the paperwork was signed and I was told to arrive first thing tomorrow morning, I bolted. It wasn't because I was scared. Definitely not because of that. But I was definitely pissed off. I knew there was a possibility of a supernatural being CEO of Solv Logistics. That was almost a given considering they employed supernaturals in the first place.

But I had no idea he was going to be a Lycan or if EH knew what he was.

I'm not sure if it was some sort of extra test my father had set up or if they had really just forgotten, but either way, I didn't like it. They let me go in missing critical information. Lacking that one piece of information could have just gotten me killed if I'd blown my cover.

Pushing the front doors, I melted into the crowded street. Even surrounded by people, out in the open, I still felt like eyes were on me. Like people already knew what I was doing and simply were waiting for their moment to strike.

Shivering, I stood on the curb, trying to hail a cab, the city busy as it always was making things like getting a taxi not that easy. After a few minutes, a yellow car sped to the curb in front of me. The cab driver dipped his head in greeting as I slid into the backseat. "Where to?"

"Madison Avenue."

He grunted in reply, pulling away from the curb and straight into traffic. My fingers tapped along the car door, anxiety curling in my stomach. A vibration in my purse made me jump. The cab driver didn't even react. Pulling out my phone, I checked the caller ID.

Dad.

"Did you get the job?" Not even a 'hello' or 'glad you're safe, honey'. His voice was as cold and emotionless as ever. To be fair, Laurent Argent raised me, so I was used to it by now. But that didn't mean I wasn't going to give him shit for it.

"Yeah, I did. No thanks to you." I leaned back against the seat, eyeing the cab driver. He was minding his own business, however. "Next time, I'd like a little more information. Like, for example, what sort of creature the CEO is."

I knew I wouldn't get all the details of every single mission. That's not how we worked. Everything was so closely guarded, even for the daughter of the head of EH. Even still, knowing what exactly I'd be dealing with seemed a bit important. Especially after all the years they had trained me to know that Lycans were among the top deadliest of supernaturals. They were uncontrollable savages and would kill without reason.

"Good. Then we can proceed to the next phase," Laurent replied dismissively. "You'll receive further instructions shortly." And with a click, he was gone.

Sighing, I slipped the phone back into my purse. It vibrated seconds later, but I didn't bother to read whatever it was he'd sent to me. I'd look it over later... perhaps with a large glass of wine and after a long hot shower. Anything to help calm the uneasy storm currently brewing inside me.

Right now, I was still irritated that he'd kept information from me, though I wasn't surprised. He'd been that way since I was born, always distant and as warm as a corpse. Not to mention a complete asshole, though sometimes I wondered if that was an inherited trait he got from my grandfather. He had a pretty big organization to run as the head of Elite Humanity, saving the world from monsters in the dark and all. So being an asshole was much needed... but I was still his daughter.

Even if he once said that family was nothing but a weakness.

At eighteen, it didn't bother me as much as it used to. I used to wish we were a normal family, living in the suburbs and having regular family dinners with some pizza rolls or some other crap like that. But, then again, if we were a normal family, we had a high possibility of getting killed by one supernatural creature or the other. I guess, knowing what I did now, I wouldn't trade it for anything in the world.

Elite Humanity gave my life a purpose. They'd honed me into a fighter who was not only meant to survive this dangerous world, but meant to help save others. Those who were unable to protect themselves because the world leaders didn't feel it justified enough to tell humanity was lurked within the shadows. Mass panic and all.

As the cab pulled up to my building, my thoughts halted. Quickly digging through my purse, I tossed a few bills onto the front seat for my fare before opening the car door. My building was beautiful and sad at the same time, home and cold all at once. A place I had to make the most of while I dreamt for something far different.

With a heavy breath, I made my way across the sidewalk towards the building. The doorman nodded as I pushed through the glass doors, pulling my keys out of my pocket. I'd argued the need for my own space as soon as I turned eighteen just to get away from my family. Not that there were many left. I was just following in my siblings' footsteps. It seemed to be a family tradition—leaving the nest as soon as we could. It didn't matter if we all still worked together, we just didn't want to live with each other anymore.

Stepping out of the elevator, I moved down the hallway towards my apartment, my keys jingling in my hand as I reached for the knob to unlock it. Of course—with my luck—the door stuck and caused me to use my shoulder to help it open. "Fucking stupid door—"

When I got the door open and flipped the light switch, I instantly froze, staring at a figure I wasn't pleased to see. "What the hell are you doing here?"

My sister leaned against the back of my couch, arms crossed. Melissa was seven years older than me, but with blonde hair and brilliant blue eyes, she looked nothing like me. Acted nothing like me as well. We couldn't be more different. Where I was chill, she was just a bitch. Arrogant. Dramatic. The eldest child in name only because her big sister personality was just non-existent.

"How did the job go?" Melissa asked, sounding exactly like our father.

"Why do you want to know?" I bit back with a snarky grin.

"Just making sure you didn't screw it up already."

Ignoring her, I head into my kitchen. Grabbing a bottle of water from my fridge, I twisted open the cap, leaning against the island counter. "I love how you think so low of me, sister."

"Did you really expect any less?" she replied tightly, face pinched as wrinkles formed across her brown line. "Everything is a joke to you."

"Careful, Melissa. All that frowning is causing wrinkles to form on your forehead, you wouldn't want that would you?" My snarky comment wasn't what she wanted to hear, and it wasn't my typical go-to. However, years of her acting the way she has toward me was quickly coming to an end. Unlike my brother, I was quicker with my comebacks to my sister.

Her... I wasn't afraid of. Patrick... well, he wasn't the easiest person to be around.

Her lips thinned in disappointment. Something she learned from dear old Laurent. "I told Father you weren't ready. That he should have sent me in instead."

I snorted. "Well, he didn't. Probably for a reason."

"What's that supposed to mean?" Her words were clipped, blue eyes narrowed.

Pushing away from the counter, I set the water bottle aside. "Why are you really here, Melissa?"

I wasn't stupid. Melissa was just one out of two older siblings and they've both been babying me my entire life. Doesn't matter that I grew up the same as them. Doesn't matter if I've been training for this my whole life, just like them. I knew they both thought Laurent giving me this mission was a huge mistake. Gritting my teeth, I waited for her carefully calculated reply.

I could tell she was holding back. "Did you get the job?"

"Of course." I couldn't hold back my grin any longer. "Did you doubt me?"

"Take this seriously, Sydney. It's not a joke. The information we got on this place…"

"What information?" I let my eyes go wide. "Oh my God, do you know something I don't know? Did you get another briefing before I did? The person actually going in?"

The sarcasm wasn't lost on her.

She pushed off the couch, face turning crimson. "Dad told me to check in on you—"

"I'm sure he did."

"—if you aren't going to be able to handle this like an adult—"

"Melissa." My fist slammed against the countertop. "I know what I'm doing. I've had the same training as you. All I have to do is gather information, not bring the company down from the inside. It's a simple mission, and I'm not going to screw it up."

Her mouth snapped shut, cheeks burning.

"Now," I said, taking another sip of water, "are you done being a bitch, or are you going to continue to jump down my throat like a psychopath?"

Melissa stepped up to the counter, fingers gripping the edge. Her eyes burned into mine. "Just don't screw this one up, Sydney. We can't afford to lose this lead."

I said nothing, but instead simply stared at her with amusement. When it was clear I wasn't going to be baited, Melissa sniffed. Turning on her heel as she headed toward the front door.

"You might want to change your locks," she glanced at me over her shoulder, "it wasn't that hard to break in here."

Rolling my eyes, I turned away tired of her dramatic nonsense. I had more important things to do than to be stood listening to her overbearing bullshit that only irritated me. If my sister had actually cared about my well being the conversation between her and I would probably had been different. But as it was, she and I didn't give to shits about each other.

As soon as the door clicked shut, I whipped around, stalking toward the door just to flip the lock back in place for good measure. I wasn't about to admit how much that actually bothered me. How my father had sent her to check on me like I was a fucking baby. With my back pressed against the door, I finally let out a frustrated groan.

When I received my first assignment, I thought it would be something cool. Something daring. Like taking out a nest of vampires that had been hunting down humans. But no. I had to be stuck with gathering information right in the lion's den, apparently. Risky, but not exactly what I'd imagined I'd be doing.

And my new boss...

Noah Solvmane was my person of interest. Whatever he had going on in his company, Elite Humanity wanted to know about it. Getting to be his secretary was the best way I'd have access to, well, everything. From the few seconds I'd met him, he'd seemed arrogant, if not reserved. And it didn't matter how hot he was with those gray eyes and dark hair, I could feel danger rolling off him in waves.

He was... something. I just didn't know what he was.

Yet.

Sighing, I pulled my phone out of my pocket. I knew I couldn't put off my father's message much longer. Whatever information he was giving me, I desperately needed. The only instructions I'd gotten so far were to apply and get the job. We never received the full mission until we needed to, just in case we were caught.

My eyes scanned the message, going back to reread it once I'd finished. It didn't seem too difficult, but it was vague as fuck.

Find any information on supernatural activity as you can.

That was it.

Hitting a few buttons, I let the virus Elite Humanity created shred the message to nothing before stuffing my phone into my back pocket. Find out anything about whatever supernatural connection that place had? For starters, they hired a crap ton of supernaturals. Hell, their head of the department was a damn vampire. And their CEO was clearly... something.

Whatever connection they're hoping I'll find, I just hope I won't get caught red-handed. If I did, not even my father would be able to help me. They had a strict agreement with these safe cities; Elite Humanity would leave the supernaturals alone as long as they weren't harming anyone. And if I broke that...

I'd be all on my own, and no one would be able to save me. The supernaturals would have every right to tear me apart.

Shivering, I pushed those thoughts aside. There was no room for fear when it came to missions. We had to think fast, act smart, and get the job done. That was it. No worrying about messing up. No fretting over the monsters that go bump in the dark.

I had one mission.

One goal.

And that's all I needed to focus on.

FIRST DAY IN HELL

SYDNEY

I stood in front of those glass doors, fingers gripping the strap of my bag until my knuckles turned white. Today was my first day as the secretary for one of the biggest logistics companies in the country. Owned by a man I knew was dangerous, and how no clue how to approach. Not that it mattered. I had a job to do.

And I would do it.

Even if it fucking killed me—not that I wanted it to.

Taking a deep breath, I forced myself to open the doors, stepping inside the spacious lobby. Cold air trickled through the vents, sending chills down my bare arms. The heat of the city evaporated as I moved toward the silver card readers. The light blinked green, and before I knew it, I stood before the elevators with a small crowd waiting to go up.

Like yesterday, there was a mix of human and supernatural. I tried to ignore the ones I knew were obviously not human, keeping my eyes straight ahead. I could feel eyes on me, however. It didn't matter if there were hundreds of workers in this company, they knew I was new.

Hell, all the training I had gone through was to fight supernaturals and being a secretary wasn't exactly something I was qualified for. So I had no doubt I had 'new girl doesn't know what the fuck she is doing' tattooed right across my forehead.

The elevator doors swished open and we stepped aside to let others filter out. I hurried in at the back of the crowd, just barely squeezing in. Trying not to get too close to one supernatural woman with golden eyes and blue hair—a Fae—that seemed intent on people watching, instead of sticking her face in her phone like everyone else.

Floor-by-floor, the elevator slowly started to empty. I was one of the very few heading up to the top. The more floors we passed, the more eyes I could feel on the back of my head.

"Is that the new secretary?" A whisper caught my attention, but I refused to turn around.

"I think so." There was a slight pause. A soft snort. "She won't last very long."

"How long did the last one make it?"

"A few months."

Chills crept down the back of my neck, though I brushed it off. Unlike the last woman, I knew what I was getting into. Somewhat. At least I was aware of the supernatural and what they were capable of. That was something the last secretary probably hadn't known. Already I was one step ahead. I just needed it to stay that way.

The gossipers stepped around me as soon as the doors opened. From their pointed ears, they were also fae. Except these were different from the woman I had noticed before. Their skin had a slight green tint to it, and their eyes were just a little too sharp. Humans wouldn't notice these types of things, but I certainly did.

They sneaked a last look before the doors slid closed, their lips moving as they whispered. I didn't hear what they said before the elevator started up to the top floor, but I didn't really care.

I had to stay focused. Today, would put me one step closer to proving myself.

When I stepped out onto my floor, I let out a heavy breath of nerves that had been building inside me all the way up to this floor. Stepping out into the lobby, I smiled at the front desk woman I'd seen yesterday. "Good morning."

She barely glanced up before looking back down at whatever she was doing. I had heard of people being rude within companies like this, but the front desk woman? That was new.

Shrugging it off, I headed through the glass doors and down the hall. My new desk sat before Noah Solvmane's office, the same as yesterday. Thankfully, his office door was closed. Which meant I had time to get situated before having to face him. Setting my purse on the floor, I tucked it beneath the drawers, prepared to dig into whatever Mr. Grey was trying to explain yesterday while I was doing paperwork.

Unfortunately for me, just as I was about to sit down and figure out my first task, the office door behind me opened.

"You're late." Noah's silver eyes narrowed. Today he wore a tight-fitting black suit with a red tie. His dark hair slicked back with a bit of stubble along his sharp jawline, giving him a more rugged look.

Glancing at the gold clock on the wall, I frowned. Mr. Grey had told me to be here at eight in the morning. It was now seven fifty-nine. "I—"

"You're to be here at seven-thirty each morning," Noah said shortly. "Check the schedule for the day. I'll need a report of all the meetings I have today within the next ten minutes." Without another word, he stepped back into his office and roughly closed the door.

I stared at where he retreated to with my lips partially opened. Clearly, there'd be no grace period to get used to things, not that I should have expected there would be. Ignoring my new boss's rudeness, I switched on the computer. It wasn't that hard to find his daily schedule. Already programmed into the computer, it popped up on the screen.

Grabbing a notepad from the middle draw and a pen from the pencil holder on top of the desk, I quickly noted his meetings for the day. I had no idea what they were for or who they were with, but it might have been something my father and Elite Humanity might be interested in. Just to be sure, I took a picture of the computer screen. Just in case.

My knuckles rapped against the glass door of Noah Solvmane's office five minutes later.

"Come in."

Pushing the door open with my shoulder, I stepped into his office. Like the rest of the building, it was minimalistic and as dark as midnight. Every piece of furniture was a smoky black with accents of gold. A large desk sat to my right, velvet black chairs sitting just before it. There was a large gold clock on the wall, the small hand slowly ticking. There were no personal pictures that I could see except one on his desk and it was turned away from the door, hidden from my view.

"Do you have the report for today?" Noah asked coldly, one eyebrow raised. It was clear he doubted my ability to keep up. Something I would have to prove to him I could do without issue, the familiar feeling of determination to prove myself growing by the minute.

"You have a nine o'clock meeting with Gregory and a twelve with Janet. There's another meeting this afternoon at two with something else scheduled for three?" I wasn't sure what that last one was since there were no names attached to it. The title had only said 'meeting'.

"Very well. Cancel the two o'clock. Reschedule that for next week." Noah's eyes slid away from me to the desktop screen to his right. His fingers flew across the keyboard, clacking keys, the only other sound in the room.

I studied him closely, trying to understand why he seemed so normal compared to the horror stories I had heard about his kind when I was younger. I had never seen a Lycan in person before, a Werewolf, yes... but Lycan's were not Werewolves. They were more monstrous creatures whose senses were ten times that of a normal shifter, and the power they held was unimaginable.

Not that we knew much about them. Lycans were rare, silent creatures.

And the worst monsters were always the ones you couldn't see coming.

"Is there anything else?" Noah asked. There was a sharpness to his words that yanked me from my thoughts.

"Uh, no. That's all."

"Then..." He motioned toward the door. "Mr. Grey will be sending up some reports later. I'll need you to make copies and put them together for me to review."

"Will do." I barely stopped myself from saluting him.

Noah's eyes cut toward me, his fingers pausing over the keyboard. Black shadows flickered around his irises as he held my gaze. This man was something else entirely, and though part of me wanted to run from his office, I couldn't move. Instead, heat rose to my cheeks as he stared at me with dangerous vibes rolling off his body.

I didn't know how to feel about it all. I was taught to fear what he was, to not try and take one on, especially alone. This was left to the elite of my people, people like my father and brother. Not that our company came across them often—in fact, I don't recall we ever had.

My heart trembled at the thought of having to be in his presence until I found out what was going on in this place. He was gorgeous, and feeling attraction to him completely threw me off balance but at the same time I was scared.

"I'll get those to you as soon as I'm done," I muttered, turning on my heel. I fled from the office, letting out a breath of relief as soon as the door shut behind me.

Noah Solvmane was a Lycan, I was sure of it. Though part of me didn't want to jump to conclusions. EH didn't have all the intel, and though it wasn't 100% known what he was, my instincts had never really been wrong before. One thing I was absolutely sure about was he was dangerous. There was an edge to him that made me nervous. For the first time, I felt out of my element. Maybe

Melissa and my brother Patrick were right, and I wasn't up to the challenge.

Maybe this wouldn't be as easy as I thought it would be.

Pushing those thoughts away, I took a seat at my desk. My phone pinged from my purse, alerting me to a message. Glancing at the office door, I dug it out from under the desk.

How is your day?

Laurent's message glared up at me. I knew he wasn't checking in on me because he cared.

Just starting, I typed quickly, keeping an eye on the office door. Knowing my luck, Noah would catch me with my phone in hand when I was supposed to be working, and then all of this would have been for nothing. My siblings would never let me live that one down.

Time's ticking.

As if I didn't know. When he'd first given me this mission, my father had been perfectly clear that the EH would need information as soon as possible. Attacks on humans in the safe cities were rising and somehow they were linked to this company. Whether Noah was the mastermind behind the attacks or if the supernaturals were planning something bigger, I didn't know.

That's why I was here.

Another sound forced my attention to the computer on my desk. An email popped up on the screen with several attachments labeled as reports. I stuffed my phone back into my bag and got to work. It took me a while to figure out where I had to print these damn things. The woman at the lobby desk wasn't very helpful in finding the copy room, but as there were only a few rooms on this floor, I found it on my own in the end.

File cabinets lined the room with a single printer set against the back wall. A black table was placed in the center of the table, made of glass. Two swivel chairs sat beside it looking forlorn. It didn't look like anyone had been in here for awhile and I wondered just how long ago it was that Noah's secretary had quit.

Papers slid out from the printer one-by-one, hot to the touch. Glancing over my shoulder, I closed the copy room door, deciding to make the most of what I was doing—and snoop. The first few pages of the reports seemed normal to me. Each one outlined each department's activities. Nothing too crazy. I didn't understand half of it, but I knew it didn't have anything to do with the supernatural. It was more about exports and imports than anything else.

Which wasn't what I was after.

Sighing, I started stacking up the papers.

"So you're the new girl."

Whipping around, I nearly dropped the stack of papers I'd grabbed from the printer. Standing in the doorway was a woman I didn't recognize but, at first glance, she looked human. Actually, she looked gorgeous. Her honey-blond hair fell in thick waves around her shoulders, freckles dotting her pale cheeks beneath brilliant blue eyes rimmed with black lashes. Her lips were painted red, her makeup subtle enough to enhance her beauty rather than diminish it. She was taller than I was, her heels giving her an extra inch.

"I—uh, yes. I guess I am." I carefully set the papers on the table, careful not to mess up their order. "Who are you?"

"Congrats. I'm Aria." She walked to the table, hand extended. I shook it warily. "I work down in Order Fulfillment."

"It's nice to meet you." I was only being nice to get her out faster. With her here, I couldn't keep going through the reports.

"First day?" Aria asked, taking a seat in one of the chairs. Inwardly, I groaned. If she insisted on staying, I'd have to come back later.

"Yes." *Please leave*, I thought. I really, really didn't want to stay here any longer than I had to.

Aria studied me, blue eyes unwaveringly innocent. "You should come out with some of us tonight. We usually go out a few times a week for drinks. It helps take the edge off."

"Edge?" The question slipped out before I could stop it.

"I mean, yeah. Working here isn't always easy." Aria grins. "And I have a feeling you'll probably need that drink sooner or later."

"Is he that bad?" I ask, nodding toward Noah's office through the glass walls. They were clouded, like his, but Aria got what I was asking about.

She shrugged. "Last girl didn't last very long. Or the one before that." There must have been a look on my face. "But who knows," she said quickly, "you might be the one that sticks around."

"Thanks," I reply dryly. "Well, I have to get these reports to Mr. Solvmane, so."

"Of course." Aria gracefully stood, hands smoothing down her bright red pencil skirt. "If you need anything, just come find me." Flashing a smile, Aria slipped out of the copy room.

I bent over the table, quickly skimming through the rest of the reports to make up for the time lost chatting to my new friend. After a few minutes, I let out a frustrated groan. There was nothing here. Nothing that EH would be interested in anyway. I couldn't end my first day without any information whatsoever, however. Which meant I'd need to stay later just to go snooping.

Perfect.

DIGGING UP DIRT

Noah

I sat in my office, listening to Sydney's conversation with one of the girls from Order Fulfillment. I hadn't meant to eavesdrop but, for some reason, I couldn't help myself. Sydney's voice had a hard edge to it, lined with control I recognized easily. She seemed reserved. Hesitant.

I couldn't blame her, I guess. She seemed more aware than the others and even they had sensed something was off about this office. The last girl had been downright terrified any time I called her name. This one, however, was different. It hadn't been fear I'd seen in Sydney's eyes this morning. It had been a challenge.

Focus.

Pushing thoughts of my secretary out of my mind, I went back to my computer. News articles filled the screen. It was all over. Another supernatural attack, though the humans didn't exactly call it that. A serial killer. Robbery gone wrong. Rabid animal. They used any excuse they could rather than face the truth.

Clicking out of the tabs, I ran a hand over my hair. The more attacks there were, the higher the risk that Elite Humanity would bring down the hammer. I needed to end this before it got out of control but, from Ace's reports, it wasn't us.

So who the hell was killing the humans?

It wasn't just in New York. From what I've gathered, there have been attacks in almost every city across the United States. My contacts have been reporting more and more rogue supernaturals. At least, that's what they thought they were. We haven't had time to talk to any of them before EH showed up and nabbed them. Every single time an attack happened, the supernatural accused would be loaded up into the back of a black van and was never seen again.

My hand scraped along my jaw, the stubble I'd forgotten to shave that morning scratching my palm. These attacks worried me. I couldn't deny they made me nervous. For years, we've had a sort of treaty with Elite Humanity. Now, everything was hanging by a thread.

Soft footsteps coming down the hall alerted me to Sydney's return. She knocked on the door softly. "Come in." I called out, preparing myself to be faced with her distracting aura again.

As the door opened, revealing stacks of papers paper-clipped together. I could barely see Sydney behind the mass amounts of white paper. Though this didn't seem to stop her in her steps as she made her way gracefully toward the desk, setting the papers at the edge. Like always, the scent of jasmine and rose filled my office, nearly suffocating me. Her emerald eyes catching mine, unafraid.

"Here are the reports you asked for," she said, motioning toward the paper. "I sorted them for you as well. They should all be in order."

My brain struggled to fight through the fog of her scent. "Thank you."

"Anything else?" she asked politely.

My eyes raked down her body. Today she wore a forest green dress that seemed to hug every curve. It matched the color of her eyes, though I'm sure she knew that. Letting my gaze trace the soft curves of her hips just a little longer before forcing myself to focus on the reports instead.

"That's all."

She said nothing as she left my office, but her presence still filled the room. It was distracting. I could hear her heart beating just outside my office, each even breath that set me further and further on edge. I couldn't focus on the reports with her around. Feeling frustrated, I tossed them aside, knowing I'd just get to them later after she left.

Sydney worked at her desk for a few more hours, though I had no idea what she was doing. I'd started off pretty easy, only requesting the meeting update and reports for this quarter that had been sent. Maybe she was familiarizing herself with the computer or messing around. I didn't know. All I knew is that her presence alone outside my door was distracting enough.

Unable to take it much longer, I pushed away from my desk and stalked out into the hall. Sydney whipped around as soon as the door opened, emerald eyes going wide.

"Why did you apply for this job?" The words were out before I could stop them.

She blinked up at me, looking confused. "Because...I needed one?"

"But why this job specifically? There are about a million and one secretarial jobs in this city." I stepped closer, eyes locked on hers.

She fidgeted in her chair a bit, fingers toying with the ends of her red hair. "I guess this was one of the first ones I saw. Is there a problem?" She didn't shy away from my scrutiny. Instead, she met my gaze with a challenging look, fire in her eyes.

"The reports weren't in the correct order." I knew I was being an ass. And I hadn't even checked the damn reports.

"Oh, well, would you like me to fix them?" she asked politely, but I could hear the slight edge to her words.

"Did you make copies?" I asked, completely ignoring her.

"Of course."

"I need you to take them down to the filing room. You should be able to figure out the system."

"Right now?"

My eyes narrowed. "Unless you have something better to do?"

"No." Her lips pursed, eyes sliding away from mine. Ignoring me, she gathered the papers on the desk, tucking them between her chest and arm before standing. "I'll get that done now before I leave for the day."

I didn't move, forcing her to brush past me on her way around the desk. There was something...off about her. I just couldn't place it. Usually, I was good at reading people. But her? She felt both like a stranger and yet not at the same time.

I watched her walk down the hall and disappear through the glass doors toward the elevator. The file room was on the floor below mine, tucked away in a corner with a scanner that only I, Mr. Grey, and my secretary could get into. After waiting for a few minutes, I went back to my desk, pulling up the security cameras.

It was pretty easy to find Sydney. She stepped off the elevator, heading down the hall toward the file room. Nothing out of the ordinary.

Leaning forward, I rested my elbows on the desk, studying her. She moved gracefully, with a strength I recognized. She might have been human, but she wasn't normal, that was for sure. Her movements were too controlled. Too purposeful.

When she reached the door, she glanced around, checking to see if anyone was watching. Her card slipped over the scanner, the light flashing green before the door unlocked. Then she was through. I switched the cameras, finding her just as she closed the door behind her. Sydney paused for a second, taking in the room before heading toward one of the long desks in the center of the room. Rows and rows of filing cabinets were stacked along the length of the room, creating a maze of black metal. We could have gone digital a long time ago, but I'd refused.

She set the reports on the table, glancing over her shoulder. I wasn't sure if she knew there were cameras in there or not, but I was intrigued to see what she'd do. Heading over to the first cabinet, she pulled out the drawer, flicking through the labeled files. Her fingers moved fast, eyes scanning the papers. I'd told her to figure out the system, but she was reading through the files as if to actually get a sense of what they were.

Unease crept through my chest, forcing me to my feet. It didn't take me long to reach the file room. I scanned my card, shoving the door open with my shoulder.

Sydney slammed one of the cabinet doors shut, whirling around. One hand flew to her chest, the other balling into a fist. "Jesus, you scared me."

"What are you doing?" I asked, stalking closer. That feeling in my chest grew, spreading through me like poison.

"Putting away the files like you asked." It was a simple enough answer. But it didn't feel right.

I eyed her warily. "If it takes you this long to complete a simple task, then don't bother. I'll have Grey do it in the morning."

Red flared across her cheeks. "I—"

"Am done for the day," I finished for her, glancing at the watch on my wrist.

Her full lips parted slightly, drawing my attention to them before I could stop myself. Thinking better of it, Sydney's mouth snapped closed. Without a word, she brushed past me, leaving the reports on the table. I closed my eyes, her scent drifting past me full blast. The unease in my chest turned sour.

I stood there in the file room for as long as I thought it would take for her to get her things and leave. For whatever reason, I didn't want to face her again after that. The way I treated her shouldn't have bothered me. But it did. I had been unreasonable, as I usually tended to be. For all I know maybe what she was doing was her way of getting familiar with things so she could put it away like I asked. But I didn't give her the chance to do that.

Running my hand over the stubble on my jawline I let out a frustrated growl that rippled from my chest. My beast was on edge every time she was around, and the fact I couldn't tell if it was because there was something wrong with her or that he liked her—irritated me further.

By the time I got to my office, even I was about done for the day. Her desk was empty and Sydney was nowhere in sight, which made me feel worse, surprisingly. Just before I reached my office door though, I paused.

Someone was inside.

Striding through the door, I found my youngest brother lounging in the chair in front of my desk. He didn't move, typing away on his phone.

"What are you doing here?" I sighed, leaning against the wall.

Glancing up from his device, the screen went black. Despite being several years younger, Lawson could have been my twin. We had the same dark hair, the same chiseled jaw and light eyes, though his were blue rather than gray. Tattoos covered his bare arms, remnants of ink inching up along his neck. He wore a cut-off leather jacket over a black t-shirt—his usual go to and so completely different from my suits.

"Updating the boss on security," Lawson replied, saluting me. I ignored that, heading for my desk. "What? No playful banter today?"

"It's been a long day," I replied evenly.

Lawson studied me, sitting up in the chair. "What's got your panties in a bunch?"

"A lot of things. Take your pick."

"I saw your new secretary before she left," Lawson whistled. "Girl's got fire in her. I can tell."

I glanced up at him sharply. "Did she say anything to you?"

"No," he chuckled, "but she was muttering about what an asshole you were while packing her things. I nearly gave her a heart attack when I came up. What's her problem?"

"Me, apparently." I leaned back in my chair, fingers locking together behind my head. "It's her first day. She'll either get used to it or quit like the last one."

Lawson rolled his eyes. "Could you at least keep this one for a few more weeks? Running background checks on every single secretary is getting old. It's probably the least exciting thing about this job."

"Yeah, well your job is about to get a whole lot more interesting," I told him.

He perked up slightly, blue eyes glowing. "Oh?"

I typed away, bringing up the news articles I'd been reading that afternoon. Turning the screen around, I made sure he could see them. "What have you heard?"

Lawson leaned forward, eyes scanning the articles. "Probably the same as you. Rogue supernaturals not following the rules." He shrugged as if that was that.

"But this many?" I asked, unable to keep the frustration from my voice. "They know the rules. They know my rules."

Lawson's gaze slid away. "Not everyone follows either."

My fist slammed against the table. "Yeah, well unless they'd like to bring EH down on all our heads, they need to."

"Let those pieces of crap come," Lawson snarled. Hatred flaring in his eyes. "It's about time we did something about them."

"Don't be stupid," I snapped in return, causing Lawson to bristle.

"So what do you need me to do?"

Catching his eye once more I sighed contemplating exactly what it was I wanted him to do. We had to be careful, because there was no doubt in my mind that EH already had people in the city trying to figure out what was going on. But at the same time, part of me wondered if they had stooped so low as to have taken part in making these attacks happen.

Nevertheless, something had to be done.

"I need you to figure out what the hell is going on, and I need you to be discreet."

LATE NIGHT INCONVENIENCES

SYDNEY

I sat there, staring at my laptop screen, finger hovering over the trackpad. I hadn't been able to get too much information today and the stuff I had gotten wasn't much. Guilt and anxiety twisted in my stomach as I hesitated, before pressing send.

I'm not sure why I felt guilty. I didn't give two craps about the company, and my new boss seemed to have a stick wedged so far up his ass he'd become numb to it. The guy might have been sinfully hot, but his attitude had ruined the looks. I felt no loyalty toward him whatsoever. Besides, it's not like Noah Solvmane screamed innocence.

And yet...

Cursing under my breath, I stabbed the enter button, sending the email to my father. Guilt aside, I knew it was the right thing to do. If something big was going on with this company—if it had anything to do with the humans being mercilessly killed—then I had to do anything and everything I could to stop it. That was my job. My duty.

My conflicting emotions had no place here.

Scrubbing a hand down my face, I let out a deep sigh. This had always been an issue for me. I knew my family had done everything they could to protect humans from the supernatural. But I also knew that not every supernatural was some evil monster. They couldn't be. Just like humans, there had to be good and bad. Yet that kind of thinking went against all of my training, all of the stories my father would tell us as kids.

Supernaturals were evil.

And humans needed to be protected.

It was simple, straightforward, and to the point. Just like most things EH did.

Unable to sit still for very long, I grabbed my purse and keys. My apartment went dark, and I made sure to switch on the extra security as I locked my door behind me. If any other siblings were going to grace me with a surprise visit, I'd know about it before I even got back.

Outside, the night had cooled off a bit, giving a brief relief to the heat of New York's summer. The crowds had subsided a bit, giving me a bit more space on the sidewalks as I headed toward my favorite restaurant. Diego's wasn't exactly top-tier, but it was greasy, delicious, and comforting. I probably went there way too much, which wasn't necessarily a good thing. If anyone knew who I truly was, they'd know where to find me. But I didn't care. Diego's double-stuffed hamburger tacos were completely worth it.

It didn't take me long to reach the hole-in-the-wall restaurant. Just a few blocks away, Diego's was pretty close. And, not that I would ever admit it, but it had been a pretty big factor when I was looking for apartments. What could I say? I was a fat kid at heart and I loved food more than anything. After a grueling day of training, I'd usually end up at Diego's to get my greasy fix of deliciousness before hating myself the next day.

Again, totally worth it.

"Look who's back." Diego grinned as soon as I stepped into the dimly lit room. He leaned against the back counter, stained apron tied around his round paunch. The few dark hairs he had left had been slicked across his bald spot, a shadow of scrub shading his thick jowls. "I was wondering when you'd come by and visit again."

"I can't stay away forever," I replied, sliding into my usual booth.

"Regular order?"

"You know me so well." My hand pressed against my chest as I blew him a kiss.

Diego disappeared into the kitchen, Spanish rolling off his tongue in quick staccato as he yelled at Juan, his only cook. Juan was just a few years older than me, but he sure knew how to make some mean meals. His cooking skills were literally to die for and if he had any sort of ambition, he could have opened up his own restaurant. But he owed Diego too much.

"So, amiga, you staying out of trouble?" Diego asked, coming back out from the kitchen before he slid into the booth across from me. The restaurant was empty, and slow for this time of night. It was times like this that Diego often sat with me as I ate. Normally I would hate the company, but I had grown used to Diego doing this and in the end, rather enjoyed the conversation.

"As much as I can," I replied. "I got a new job."

Diego's eyebrow arched. "Oh? And what are you doing now?"

He didn't know what I really did for a living, and I'm pretty sure he knew nothing about the supernatural, but I'd always kept him updated on what I was doing. "I'm the new secretary for Solv Logistics."

Diego let out a low whistle. "¡Qué impresionante! Didn't know you were into those big Fortune 500 deals."

"I'm not." I snorted, my finger tracing old scars along the table-top. "My dad's idea."

"Ah." Understanding washed over his face. "You know, our parents always want what's best, but it might not always be the best thing for us. If I'd listened to my father, I'd still be out west workin' on cars rather than here living the dream, you know?"

I couldn't keep the grin off my face. "Thank God for that. I'd die without your tacos. They're the only thing that gets me through the week."

"Makes me happy to hear." Diego rapped his knuckles on the table. "They'll be out in a minute. Do you want to stay or to go?"

"I have to take it back home," I replied with regret. "Have some work to catch up on."

Diego nodded in understanding. "I'll get that right out to you."

True to his word, Diego delivered my doggy bag in just a few minutes. I paid and thanked him before slipping out the door. Shadows clung to every building as I headed back to my apartment. Usually, I wasn't afraid of the night because I knew what stalked in the darkness, but something felt off tonight. A chill rolled down my spine as I tucked my bag of food under one arm. Pulling out my phone, I checked my messages just in case my father had replied.

He had.

Is this it?

Short and sweet, but I could just imagine the disappointment behind his words. Feeling frustrated, I typed out my reply, telling him that it was only my first day—not that he would care—and that the boss was a bit more overbearing than I'd thought he'd be. I hadn't counted on him following me to the copy room. That hadn't seemed like something a CEO would even care to check in on. Clearly, he'd been watching me over the cameras, which seemed a bit paranoid to me, but hey—what did I know?

I'll get more information soon.

My eyes were glued to the phone as I walked, anxiously waiting for a reply.

Better get it fast.

Thank you, Dad. It's not like I wanted to stay at that job for longer than I had to. Solv Logistics was crawling with supernaturals and, sooner or later, my cover could be blown one way or another. I needed to figure out if Noah and his people had anything to do with the killings going on, and I needed to figure that out fast. If they were... well, it wouldn't look good to have an EH operative infiltrating their company.

"You lost sweetheart?"

Shit.

I stashed my phone in my pocket, glancing up to find two rather intimidating men standing in my way. I didn't recognize the street, which meant I'd probably taken a wrong turn when I wasn't paying attention.

Double shit.

"Nope." I eyed them warily, trying to make out their features through the shadows. The alley I'd turned on wasn't lit very well. But I knew right away they weren't human. There was a chill in the air, a heavy feeling that my gut couldn't ignore. "Excuse me."

The one on the right was thick, with arms that looked like they could crush my windpipe in seconds. His hair was dark, the color of midnight, and shaved close to his scalp. Thick hair covered his arms, peeking out from under the t-shirt and leather jacket he was wearing. The one on the right was slimmer, but equally terrifying. His hair was lighter, the color of straw. Both of them had a strange glint in their dark eyes.

"Excuse her," the one on the left said, voice rising to mock me. His buddy laughed, his voice sending shivers skittering along my skin.

My eyes narrowed. "Are we really going to do this?"

"That depends, sweetheart," Lefty replied, grinning. Two sharp fangs pricked his lower lip.

Not vampires. Their skin was too bronze to be dead. If the hair was anything to go by, I would assume werewolf.

"On?" My doggy bag dropped to the ground, my irritation spiking. If they made me lose the dinner I'd been looking forward to all week, I was going to be more than pissed.

"If you're looking to have some fun."

Righty moved first. I ducked, rolling underneath his brutish arms. Lefty's claws swiped through the air, catching my shirt. I heard the fabric rip as I jerked away. My movements were clumsy, and I knew it. Swearing, I fumbled for the knife I kept in the sheath strapped to my stomach.

But I was too slow.

Gasping, my fingers clawed at the hand currently choking the life out of me. I could feel my nails raking across Righty's skin, but he was too strong. His black eyes glowed as he laughed, his fingers squeezing harder until spots danced across my vision.

"Not so tough now," he growled. His lip curled, revealing two lethal canines.

I tried to lash out with my knee, aiming for that sweet spot. Supernatural or not, they still had their weaknesses. He blocked it easily, ripping the knife out of my hand in the process. Lefty caught my only weapon in midair, looking it over.

"This girl's got some claws of her own," Lefty observed, "And she doesn't seem too surprised."

"Get your dirty claws off me," I snarled. Or, at least tried to. It's a little hard to sound intimidating when life was slowly being squeezed out of you.

"I don't think so." Righty leaned in closer. His breath smelled like rotting meat and dried blood. My stomach dropped, my vision fading at the edges.

Over his shoulder, something dark caught my eye. At first, I thought it was just a shadow. But then it moved. My mouth opened in warning, ice freezing my limbs in place. Whatever the hell that thing was, it wasn't good. The temperature dropped, the blood pounding in my ears as I watched the monster draw closer. I didn't know whether to warn Lefty or Righty or watch them get torn to pieces by... whatever that thing was.

Then again, it would probably rip me apart as well.

Righty seemed to finally notice I wasn't paying much attention to him. He glanced over his shoulder, catching sight of the blasted thing I'd noticed far sooner. Swearing, his grip around my neck loosened. Lefty swung around, my knife raised in warning.

But he wasn't fast enough.

With a scream, Lefty disappeared into the darkness, dragged along the ground. A snarl cut through the air, bone-chilling and emotionless, overpowering the terrified cries of the werewolf. Righty swore again. I felt his hand come free, but I wasn't prepared for it.

My body hit the ground with a hard thud, my head cracking against the pavement. Pain shot through me, radiating down every limb, every nerve. My vision went white before fading to black. I could barely see a thing. But I heard it all. The tearing. The ripping.

The screams.

My head lolled to the side, my body too broken to move. To run.

And then... the alley fell silent.

The shadow moved as fear constricted around my lungs until I couldn't breathe... I couldn't move. A snarl pierced through the silence. A warning of what was to come.

And before I knew it... everything went dark.

BACK ALLEY ATTACK

NOAH

~One Hour Earlier~

Late nights at the office weren't anything new to me. Lawson had stayed, helping me comb through information as we tried to piece together with what the fuck was going on in our city. None of what we found out ending up being helpful though. The newspapers would claim it was anything but what it actually was, so we were forced to read between the lines. A car accident where the victim had bled to death—Vampire. An wild dog attack—Werewolf. Strange death no one could explain? More than likely Fae.

Eventually, even I was forced to give up. We could decipher which supernatural did the killings, but we still couldn't figure out why. There was no motive behind them. The attacks were in cities that had resources for us, like blood and raw meat. There was no reason for these supernaturals to kill for food.

It didn't make sense.

"We're getting nowhere," Lawson growled, tossing another printed paper onto my desk. It was cluttered with reports and news articles, with more being printed off as he spoke. "I hate to say this, but maybe there isn't some conspiracy behind these killings. Maybe they're just getting tired of Elite Humanity's rules."

I cast him a sharp look showing my irritation. "They know the rules and they know what Elite Humanity will do if they're caught. And, so far, they've all been caught." I stopped short, the realization hitting me like a sack of bricks. "They've all been caught."

Lawson eyed me warily. "Yeah...? Elite Humanity didn't manage to be the top supernatural police force by letting us go, bro."

Police force? That was a laugh. They thought they were but they weren't. They were a group of sadistic hunters who gave themselves a title to make themselves feel better about what they did to us.

"No." He wasn't getting it. I pulled up the search engine on my laptop. "You and I both know that there are thousands of deaths by supernaturals a year. Most are caught by Elite Humanity and are dealt with. Many are not."

"So maybe Elite Humanity's just stepped up their game."

"There's been about forty-five deaths in the past few months alone from these reports," I muttered. "All of the arrests have been one after another. They're good, but not that good."

"So, what are you thinking?" Lawson asked, frowning.

"I don't know." Frustration flickered in my chest. "Yet."

"Well, we're not going to solve this little problem tonight," Lawson said, sighing. "And I'm starved. Can we please go? Because, unlike you, I don't live at the office."

"Fine." I replied as I started gathering up the papers, stacking them neatly on top of my desk. Lawson, though, simply tossed the papers he'd been holding, knocking over my stack. "Seriously?" I snapped, gritting my teeth as I fixed them again.

Lawson simply scoffed as he shook his head, making his way towards the door. He didn't care that he was annoying me, in fact—he lived for it. Grabbing my jacket, I stood to my feet and followed Lawson out the door, flicking the lights off behind us. The office was deadly quiet at this time of night. Everyone else had gone home long ago, but this wasn't unusual for me. I liked the office like this. No one bothered me with stupid questions or pointless small talk. Not that many of my staff talked to me in the first place. They knew better than that.

"What are you thinking tonight?" Lawson asked, pressing the elevator button. "You up for a little fun?"

Shaking my head, I frowned. "Not tonight."

I knew what he was aiming for, and though we let our beasts out on occasion... I couldn't help but feel I was needed for something else tonight. Something important I couldn't miss. Even the beast that lurked beneath my skin didn't jolt at the idea to have fun, instead he seemed still—calm even.

My younger brother eyed me as the elevator doors opened and we stepped inside. "You haven't shifted with me in forever. Come on, Noah. I might think you don't like me anymore."

"I'm sure you're fine," I replied blandly.

"Have you talked to Shane recently?" Lawson asked, changing the subject. We watched as the lights over the numbers in the elevators slowly flashed with each passing floor.

"No." My other brother wasn't one to call me for casual conversations. His personality was a bit more like me—but he had a family... something I'd never partake in. "You?"

Lawson nodded a bit. "Yeah, sure. He's still out in bloody Australia with his kids. They've gotten big. You really should talk to him soon."

"I will," I replied, not that it was easy to talk to him. I felt bad for my brother. My mate had been taken from me, but his—she left him and their children. Every time I spoke with him it reminded me of the family I would never have.

We fell silent as the doors swished open to reveal the empty lobby. One of Lawson's guys manned the front desk and as soon as he saw us, he straightened, nodding in respect. At this time of night, the city was still alive. People scurried down the sidewalks, heading out to their bars and parties for the evening. Most supernatural beings liked the cities because it was easier to hide from the humans in plain sight.

I liked it for another reason.

"You calling for your driver?" Lawson asked.

When we stepped onto the sidewalk, the cool night air touched my skin, causing me to close my eyes as I inhaled the fresh scent of night. "No. I think I'll walk tonight." Glancing at him, I raised a brow. "Walk with me?"

Lawson shrugged. "It's not like I have anything better to do tonight," he muttered.

We started down the sidewalk, the humans parting for us like the Red Sea. They might not know what we were, but they certainly knew to stay away. Unlike other supernaturals, it was harder for me to blend in. I knew I stood out. I knew the power I radiated. I wasn't trying to hide it.

"So how's the new secretary working out?" Lawson asked casually. "I know I mentioned her earlier, but you didn't really say much."

Emerald-green eyes instantly popped into my mind, and I tried hard to shove the image away just as quickly as it had come. "She'll do for now."

Lawson gave a low whistle. "Wow. High praise from you, that is. I distinctly remember you calling the last secretary a—what was it? A complete degenerate who would have made Darwin turn in his grave?" His lips twisted into a shit-eating grin that made me roll my eyes.

"I do sometimes still wonder if she's still alive," I remarked casually.

"This one seems to have a head on her," Lawson said. "Though I wouldn't blame her if she just didn't show up tomorrow."

A frown tugged at the corners of my lips just thinking of the possibility. "I'm not that bad."

"Whatever you say."

I was about to reply when we heard a short scream. It wasn't close, maybe a few blocks away, but it was clear enough to us. Lawson paused, one foot raised mid-step, as we listened. I recognized that voice almost immediately, despite only hearing it a few times.

Sydney.

"What—"

I didn't wait for Lawson. Slipping into an alley, I raced between buildings, keeping to the shadows. Sounds of struggling mixed with the usual noises of the city. Metal clicked—maybe a knife.

The closer I got, the more I could make out. Sydney's gasping breath, the sound of her nails scratching along skin in a frenzy.

I sensed them before I saw them.

Lawson nearly smacked into me as I froze, assessing the scene. The men I didn't recognize, but I could smell what they were.

Werewolves.

"Are they—?"

I growled, cutting my brother off. "No."

"Then it's not our problem. Elite Hum—"

Ignoring him, I started tugging at the knot of my tie. I felt the change take over almost immediately. My beast slipped over my skin like water, raising the hair along the back of my neck. Bones cracked, like stretching after a long day. I didn't care if my clothes were dumped on the dirty New York grounds, and I didn't give a shit about anyone finding them.

All I knew was that Sydney was in danger.

A growl ripped through my throat as I stalked forward, slipping into the alley. The two Werewolves hadn't sensed me yet. They were too intent on their prey. But she did.

Her eyes caught mine over one of her attacker's shoulders, though there was no way she'd recognize me. His hand gripped her throat, slowly squeezing the air from her lungs. I could practically taste her fear. Her anger. She tried to kick the man holding her; her nails leaving raw marks along his wrist and hand.

I didn't care if I was outnumbered. All my beast and I knew was that she was in danger. That... and that we had to protect her.

Snarling, I stalked forward. I was far bigger than they were. Standing on two legs, I towered over the other two men with a height that was just over seven-feet tall. Even if they had time to shift, it wouldn't matter. I was far bigger and faster than they were.

Lunging forward, my claws lashed out, snatching one of the men by the shoulder. My nails dug into his skin as I yanked him back, dragging him into the darkness. He barely had time to scream, his vocal cords torn from his throat in seconds. The other Werewolf whirled around as he dropped Sydney in the process.

I heard her head crack against the cement, a gasp escaping her lips as her body hit the ground. It was second nature to me as I ripped through the last man standing in my way. He had hurt Sydney and because of that he had to die. I pressed forward—he didn't stand a chance, not even a scream had time to register from his throat as I ripped him limb from limb.

By the time Lawson showed up, I'd changed back, blood staining my lips, my hands, my chest. It was everywhere, the scent nearly overpowering.

But not as strong as hers.

Jasmine and roses hung in the air of the small alleyway, making my head light. It was hard to think, hard to push the beast back inside me. He wanted nothing more than to stay here by her side, to comfort and protect her. Which made absolutely no sense to me.

"Jesus Christ," Lawson muttered as I shifted back. He passed me my clothes, waiting for me to dress before going to check out Sydney. From her breathing, she was out cold, but I didn't hear anything that should have been concerning. "Isn't this your secretary?"

I said nothing. A glint of metal caught my eye. It was a small switchblade, clearly belonging to her. I slowly buttoned up my shirt, red staining the fabric. My fingers brushed against the handle, picking it up. It was delicate yet sturdy, deadly, and inconspicuous. Small enough to be tucked beneath clothing, which is where I assumed she'd kept it.

My finger slid along the edge of the blade, the pain so intense I nearly dropped it.

It was made of pure silver.

Why the hell would a young secretary think to carry around a silver blade?

"Noah." Lawson's voice pulled me out of my thoughts. "She doesn't look too good." He glanced up at me, warily. "What should we do with her?"

"Call Shannon. Get her address."

"Shannon from HR?" he asked with confusion in his tone.

Flicking the blade back into its sheath, I tucked it into my pocket before kneeling, my arms slipping beneath Sydney's body as I hauled her up. "Do you know another Shannon in my company?"

Muttering, Lawson pulled out his phone and dialed her number. I wasn't sure why he would want to test my patients at a time like this, but staring down at the woman in my arms, I found myself calm around her, yet my beast was incredibly concerned.

Minutes later, Lawson came back. "She lives nearby."

"Good," I replied, motioning for him to take the lead.

"You're just going to take her home? Don't humans usually need to go to the hospital or something?"

My eyes narrowed at his comment. "They'll ask too many questions. And unless you'd like to bring Elite Humanity down on our heads, then she's not going. We're taking her home."

He knew the severity of the situation, and I wasn't sure what I was going to do but deep down, I did know I couldn't just leave her here. There was no telling if she would be okay, and not knowing that ate away at my soul.

Lawson took us around the block down Madison Avenue. I had no idea how such a young woman who just got a job could afford such a place, but it wouldn't surprise me if she lived off her family's money. I suppose what did catch me off guard was that she didn't seem like the type of woman who would do something like that.

"This is it." Lawson glanced up at the apartment. My eyes cast around the area, taking note of those who may have been watching. Per usual with these kinds of buildings there was a doorman at the front, keeping watch.

A problem that would need to be taken care of.

"Take care of him," I said, nodding toward the man. I didn't want anyone seeing us. They'd ask too many questions. Who wouldn't? I was carrying an unconscious woman to an apartment building.

"Got it, boss," Lawson replied, giving me a mock salute, "her apartment is on the top floor. The penthouse."

While my brother distracted the doorman, I slipped by them easily enough. I didn't get far enough into her apartment before Sydney began to stir in my arms. We took the elevator up to the top floor. Her lashes fluttered against her cheeks and for the first time since we'd met, I was able to study her.

Even asleep, she looked beautiful. Thick black lashes lined her eyes, leading down to a small, button nose. This close, I could see a smattering of freckles across her cheeks that I hadn't noticed before. Her full lips were parted slightly, her breath even and deep.

She was perfect in every way. A goddess, simply hidden within the body of a human woman. A woman who drove my beast and I to the brink of insanity—and we had only just met. Trying to ignore the weight of her body against my chest, I stepped out of the elevator and towards her apartment. There was much I wanted to know, and questions I needed answers to but all of it would have to wait. The only thing that mattered right now was her.

She was safe.

For now.

New Friends and Family

Sydney

My throat burned. Head pounding, even a slight groan sent pain radiating down my body. It felt like I'd jumped from the top of my apartment building to the cement, and yet had still managed to survive. With aching muscles, I peeked one eye open, hissing when I looked straight into a ray of sunshine filtering in through my window.

Wait.

Ignoring the pain, I bolted upright, head spinning. I was in my bedroom, still dressed in the same clothes as the night before. Something was wrapped around my throat, rustling as I moved. My fingers brushed against the gauze sitting just above my shirt collar.

What the fuck happened? How did I get here?

I couldn't remember anything. Everything was hazy. Holding my head, I turned to dangle my legs over the edge of the bed as I looked around. Nothing seemed out of the ordinary, at least not that I could see. But then how had I gotten home?

Standing to my feet a bit unsteady, my head dizzied to the point of stars flashing across my vision. I halted, trying to get a sense of my surroundings before I ended up on the ground again. I didn't even remember how I got away from the two Werewolves. All I remembered was being unable to breathe before everything went black.

No. That's not right.

I remember seeing another shadow.

Dark eyes flecked with gold.

Another werewolf, possibly, though it wasn't like any I'd seen before. There was something different about it. Darker. A true monster.

Had it... saved me? Or had I somehow gotten away on my own and I just didn't remember?

My hand flew to the sheath under my shirt, where I kept my switchblade. It wasn't there anymore. A bit frantic, I glanced around my bedroom before finding it on the small table next to my bed. Nearly running to it, I swept it up and pressed it against my chest.

I'd been taken by surprise last night and it had almost cost me my life. I should have been more careful. I should have paid more attention. There were a lot of should'vs I probably missed, but those were the two biggest ones. Being raised in EH my whole life, I knew better than to not pay attention to my surroundings. I'd been stupid.

And there was no way in hell I was reporting that to my father. If he or my siblings ever got wind of it, I'd never be able to go out on a mission on my own ever again. I would have proved them all right—that I wasn't ready to do this, even though I've never felt more ready in my life.

With the exception of last night, of course.

"God, how could I have been so stupid..." I grumbled.

Anxiety spiked through me at the small flashes of memories. I didn't remember much, but it was enough to leave my palms slick with sweat and my mouth dry. For the first time since I'd taken this mission, it all felt so real. Trying to distract myself, I glanced at the time.

Crap.

Stumbling to my closet, I grabbed the first things I saw before throwing them on. I slipped leggings beneath a plain white blouse, slinging a black, cropped jacket over that. Before I stuffed my feet into some black flats as I ran to the bathroom. I barely had time to brush my teeth and throw on some concealer and mascara to hide the type of night I'd had.

"Fuck... I look like shit."

Staring at my reflection, I caught the faint hint of marks around my neck. They weren't that noticeable, and if I kept my hair down, then hopefully my boss wouldn't notice them either.

Glancing at a clock, I took note of the time, and let out a frustrated groan again. I didn't have time to waste trying to hide what had happened to me. The only thing I could do was make the most of my situation and pray to whatever gods were out there that I'd not get in trouble for my appearance or possibly being late.

It took a bit longer to get a cab than I thought, which meant I was walking through the front doors of Solv Logistics with no time to spare. Hurrying through the crowded lobby, I kept my head down. Even without looking, I knew I was surrounded by supernaturals. Goosebumps slipped down my arms as I hurried through the turnstile and toward the elevators.

I could feel eyes on me. I always felt eyes on me.

Glancing up, I met the gaze of a Fae. His lips quirked to the side in a greeting that sent my heart racing again. And not in a good way. I turned away from him, only for my eyes to land on a Vampire right in front of me. Images of the Werewolves flickered through my mind over and over. The feeling of its hand around my neck felt all too real. I could practically feel the pricks of its claws digging into my skin.

Jesus Christ, Sydney. Get your shit together, woman. You've got this!

By the time I made it to my desk, I was sweating. I sank into my chair, taking deep, slow breaths to slow my heart rate down while the computer booted up.

"Are you alright?"

I jumped a little, whipping around toward the office door. Noah stood there, hands in his pockets, watching me. There was a look on his face I couldn't quite decipher. Curiosity, maybe. Genuine concern? But that wouldn't make any sense.

"Yeah, I'm fine." I turned back to the computer, finding the calendar for the day. "I'll have a report of your meetings in just a bit."

"Take your time," Noah replied, voice softer than what I was accustomed to.

I swallowed, unsure of how to react to that. He'd been concerned yesterday when he'd thought I'd been late by a minute. Yet he didn't say a word about it today. I waited for him to go back into his office before I started work, however it took him longer than

I expected before he finally closed the door, and I was left on my own.

I was paranoid the entire day. Any time a supernatural glanced my way, a spike of fear would instantly slash right through me. Aria found me at lunch, dragging me down to the company's cafeteria despite my protests. I gave in, but only because I hadn't eaten breakfast that morning, let alone a cup of coffee. Not to mention, I really needed something to preoccupy my mind.

"You can meet the rest of the Solv crew," Aria said, her arm looping through mine as we took the elevator down to the basement. "There are some great people here."

At least those great people were all human.

"This is Clara," Aria motioned toward a woman with glasses that made her eyes look too much like an owl's, "and David." David was a scrawny guy that definitely looked like he worked in some tech area. "And Adam."

Adam glanced up as she said his name, his blue eyes meeting mine. They were a startling color, though not nearly as impressive as Noah's. His smile was easy-going and, with his blonde hair and scruff, he gave off major Golden Retriever energy.

"It's nice to meet you." He held out his hand, shaking mine. "What do you do here?"

"She's the boss's new secretary," Aria announced proudly. She took a seat next to Clara, leaving the only open chair for me beside Adam. I slid into it, feeling less anxious than before.

The cafeteria was pretty impressive. Despite being in the basement, one side was made up of all windows, leading out onto a back patio of sorts with stone fountains and a small garden. Inside, different stands lined the other walls that had everything from

Mexican to Thai, coffee to tea. It was like a mall's cafeteria but fancier somehow. The tables were all black wood with matching chairs. A few red velvet booths were thrown in at the center of the room, a row of potted plants in between.

"What do you want?" Aria asked, turning to me. "I'll grab it for you. You must be super busy up there and probably could use a break."

I let out a soft sigh of relief. "Just a coffee for now. I forgot to grab one this morning."

Clara grimaced. "Jesus. Working without coffee? I don't know how you're even sitting up right now."

"That's because not all of us survive on caffeine," Adam replied, tipping his smoothie toward hers. It looked like some healthy, green concoction. I sat there, listening to them go back and forth for a bit. It all seemed so... normal. They weren't scared or paranoid, despite being surrounded by supernaturals. Which was probably due to them not even knowing they existed, but still. It felt nice to be around people that weren't constantly looking over their shoulder or afraid of having their throat ripped out by some monster with overly large canines.

"So what's it like?" David asked, glancing over at me.

"What's what like?" I hadn't been paying too much attention to their conversation.

"Working for Noah Solvmane," he replied with a goofy smile, seeming genuinely curious about what my boss was like. Which was odd because I would have assumed most had met him over their time working here.

"Have you met him?" Clara whispered.

I frowned. "Of course. It would be kind of hard to be his secretary if I never met him." They glanced at each other and I had a feeling that they didn't really see him that much. "Have you met him?"

"I've seen him come into work sometimes," Clara replied. "But I've never talked to him. I'm in production management, so we don't really interact."

"And I'm just the tech guy, so I never see him at all," David added. "Apparently, his computer never has an issue."

Adam snorted. "He's not like some mysterious celebrity. He's just like any of us."

"Except super hot and definitely mysterious," Clara argued. "His family built up this entire company from scratch and have maintained it for generations. Usually, there'd be some scandal by now or some errant son that screws everything up and neither has happened."

"Well, maybe they're just a very put-together family," Adam replied. "I don't know. The guy seems like he has a stick up his ass whenever I see him walking around."

I couldn't argue with that, but Noah's words to me this morning echoed in my ears. He'd seemed genuinely concerned. Or maybe I'd just imagined it because he couldn't possibly know what had happened to me last night.

My phone vibrated, pulling my attention away from the conversation.

Reports. Now.

It wasn't a saved contact, but I knew who it was.

Groaning internally, I knew I couldn't put off messaging him back. I had to give him what he wanted and standing at my feet, I decided to do just that. "I have to get back to work, but it was nice meeting you all."

"Where ya headed?" Adam asked, tossing his smoothie into the trash along with my cup.

"The copy room. There are still some reports I still have to file." I stood awkwardly, watching him as he pushed his chair in.

"I'll come with you. I have to pick something up for my department, anyway." He shot me an easy smile, motioning for me to go out first. I wasn't sure what it was about this guy, but something about him was slightly comforting. We walked to the elevator doors in silence, having him there made me feel slightly less paranoid.

Slightly.

As we headed up to the copy room, Adam shifted beside me. He seemed like he wanted to say something before thinking better of it. It wasn't until we actually got to the copy room that he spoke up catching me completely off guard.

"So, I know we just sort of met and you're new here and every-thing," his hand rubbed the back of his neck, "but I was wondering if maybe you'd want to grab a coffee sometime?"

Glancing at him in surprise, I swiped my card. "Like... a date? Or?"

"I guess, yeah." He replied, his cheeks flushed slightly, head dip-ping as he opened the door for me. I was taken aback by the gesture, unsure of what to say. So instead of replying, I simply kept quiet. I wouldn't be in this place long enough for a good guy like him to get to know me. The last thing I wanted to do was give the guy the wrong impression.

Slipping inside, I tried to process his offer. "I'm not sure that's a good idea, Adam."

"Why not?" he replied, staring at me with confusion. "It's just coffee."

It was just coffee, but I didn't want him to get the wrong idea. "Look, your offer is sweet and all but I just got here, and I'm not looking to go out with anyone. I appreciate the offer though."

I hoped the conversation would be over, but from the look on Adam's face, he didn't seem like someone who had been rejected before. "Seriously?"

"Yeah, I'm sorry... but it's a no for me."

Turning away from him, I made my way towards the filing cabinet. However, I didn't get far before the door slammed, startling me. "Look, just come out... you never know, you may enjoy yourself."

A grasp at my wrist threw my mind into a whirlwind and without thinking, I swung back and punched Adam in his mouth. I hadn't meant to hit him like that. It was second nature. However, the guy had it coming. Golden retriever or not... I had said no, and he was pressing the issue. Adam's blue eyes were wide with surprise as he stared up at me, open-mouthed.

The faint sound of the door to the filing room opened and brought me back to reality. The footsteps of a newcomer echoed around us. "Sydney?"

I muttered apologies under my breath. Heat flared across my cheeks as I glanced up, my eyes meeting Noah's.

Crap.

My eyes turned back to Adam, who held his jaw, glaring at me with anger. "What the hell?"

"I said I was sorry, Adam," I replied, "I told you no, and you didn't listen."

Noah glanced indifferently between the two of us registering no emotion over what had happened. It probably didn't look good for his secretary to attack his workers in the copy room. Not that it was intentional or anything. But still, he showed no emotion.

"Sydney... can you come with me, please?" Noah said, my eyes casting towards the floor as I realized how badly I had just fucked up.

"Yeah..." I replied softly. I had royally screwed up.

ALTERCATIONS & HEATED MOMENTS

NOAH

Sydney was quiet the entire ride up to my office. She wouldn't look at me, her eyes locked onto her feet as we headed down the hall. I had no idea what to say to her. Clearly, she had to have remembered something from last night. She'd been jumpy all day, her eyes darting down the hall every five seconds when she was at her desk.

I'd been keeping an eye on her just to make sure she was alright. And to see if she remembered anything. Not many humans knew about us, and I wanted to keep it that way. Elite Humanity was enough to deal with as it were, and I didn't need any more humans grabbing their torches and pitchforks.

I could feel her fear though. It rolled off her in waves. I'd been watching her since she'd walked through those front doors today, noting the way she eyed certain workers as she got on the elevator, the way she seemed to have shrank as it slowly made its way to the top floor. She'd been walking on eggshells all morning, tentatively staying out of everyone's way—both human and supernatural.

Something felt off with the way she was acting. Sure, it might have been normal for someone who'd just been attacked, but I couldn't help but feel as if maybe she knew exactly what had happened last night. As if she knew, those two men weren't entirely human at all.

Which would have been insane.

Only Elite Humanity and a select few knew of our existence. If she was one of them, I would have known about it, but it also made me think that maybe I didn't know her at all. She seemed like a normal human girl. Yet that move in the copy room was too well-practiced. Too concise. Either she'd been taking self-defense lessons since she was a kid, or there was something more to her than I'd thought.

Once we were finally in my office, I motioned for her to take a seat in the chairs across from my desk before I sank into my office chair, studying her. There were still marks on her neck, though they were faint. I'm sure she noticed them this morning, however. I just didn't know how much she remembered.

Though she must have remembered something, because otherwise, why would she be afraid like she was? Why would she be on edge?

Sydney still wouldn't look at me as she sat there, her gaze on the edge of my desk. Her fingers twisted in her lap nervously. I wasn't used to this Sydney. She'd been unafraid of me the first time we'd met, but now she couldn't even meet my gaze.

"Can you explain what happened in the copy room?" I asked quietly. My fingers laced together, resting atop the desk.

Her gaze snapped up to meet mine, and I was surprised to find fire in her eyes, not fear. "What happened was that a coworker grabbed me without consent, and I reacted without thinking. That's all."

"Grabbed you without consent?" That wasn't exactly what I expected to hear. Anger flared in my chest. "What do you mean? Did he touch you?"

As soon as I saw them head toward the copy room together, I'd been on the move. It wasn't like I expected anything to happen. But Adam had certainly seemed a little too friendly toward her in the cafeteria. Not that I was stalking her because I wasn't. I just wanted to make sure last night hadn't sent her into some downward spiral of insanity.

It took her a second to realize what she'd said. "Not like that," she replied quickly. "He just grabbed my hand, and I wasn't expecting it."

"You can't just hit people for grabbing your hand." I frowned.

"So you're saying I can't protect myself in the workplace?" she shot back, one eyebrow arching. "That seems like an HR disaster waiting to happen."

"That's not what I meant," I growled. She was purposely being frustrating. She knew exactly what I was talking about. "I meant, it's not a usual reaction to hit someone for grabbing your hand."

"Maybe not for you."

"Sydney."

She glared up at me. "Sydney what? He wouldn't get the hint that I didn't want to go out with him and he took me by surprise, and that's that. I didn't do it on purpose." I could feel her anxiety. She was struggling with more than just Adam cornering her in the copy room. That I would have to deal with later, but for right now, my sole attention was on her.

She had to be terrified. If she didn't know about supernaturals, then her brain was probably trying to come up with every excuse under the moon as to what had happened. Maybe she believed she'd just been mugged, though I'd made sure nothing was taken from her. That was a pretty plausible excuse for New York.

"Did something happen to make you feel uncomfortable?" I tried to make my words sound as soft as possible, but they still came out sounding like a growl.

She hesitated, fear slipping across her face too quickly for me to register it at first. "No," she said finally, the emotion gone just as quickly as it had come. "I've just been a bit jumpy today."

"Why?" I wanted her to come out and tell me what she remembered from last night. I needed to know if she remembered what truly happened.

If she remembered me.

"No reason."

I leaned back in my chair, eyes narrowing. Fine. If she wanted to play games, then we'd play. "Adam's a hard worker," I said, hands locked behind my head. "He's a good guy, from what I hear around the office. From what I saw, you just attacked one of my workers for no reason."

Anger sparked in her eyes. "Attacked?" she scoffed. "I barely touched him."

"Sydney, you just hit him in my copy room."

"You're being overly dramatic."

"Am I?" I stood, leaning over my desk. Sydney mirrored my movements until our faces were just inches away, the fire never leaving her eyes.

"Yeah, you are. I'm just trying to do my job, not get hit on by my co-workers." Her eyes narrowed, daring me to challenge that.

"Well, if you feel there's an issue, you can always fill out a complaint with HR," I replied evenly. My eyes darted from hers down to her lips before flicking back up. I could practically feel the heat wash over her, tingling her cheeks. The smell of her arousal overpowered her usual scent, making my head feel light.

She tried to hide it, though not very well. Her teeth grazed her bottom lip, drawing my eyes back down. There's nothing between us but electricity singing the air. If I touched her now, I knew my fingertips would burn. As would the rest of me.

Her emerald eyes flashed, lashes blinking rapidly as she pulled away. "How did you even get my number, anyway?"

"What?" The change of conversation took me by surprise.

"You texted me just a few minutes ago about the reports." She studied me carefully, eyes narrowed in suspicion. "I didn't put my personal cell phone on the application or staff records. So, how did you get my phone number?"

I walked around my desk, unable to look away from her. "You must have given it at some point."

We were inches away again, her head tipped back to hold my stare. "I know I didn't."

A low rumble rolled through my chest. "You're my secretary," I murmured, hand lifting to tuck a stray curl behind her ear. "Of course, I would have your number. If you didn't give it to me, then I probably had someone look it up. This is New York, sweetheart. It's not that hard."

I couldn't tell her the real reason for how I'd gotten her number. I hadn't gone through her phone out of respect for her privacy, but

I also didn't feel comfortable leaving without making sure I had a way of getting a hold of her. Just in case. Her human brain would try to rationalize it, just like it would with the attack.

"So you're stalking me now?" she breathed. Her eyes flicked down to my mouth, the scent of her arousal becoming almost overpowering. But there was an edge to her words.

I was scaring her.

Good, I thought. I should scare her.

But that didn't make me feel any better.

My fingers brushed against her cheek, sparks igniting against my skin. Sydney's breath caught, her eyes going wide. Before I could say another word, a wall came up, blocking me out. Without looking at me, she brushed past me, her shoulder grazing mine on her way to the door.

"Sydney."

She froze with one hand on the handle. Her shoulders tensed as if expecting the worst.

"You never got those reports. I still need them filed."

"I'll get it done," she muttered, throwing the door open.

"One more thing," I called out. She paused in the doorway, waiting. "Make a complaint with HR next time instead of punching my coworkers in the office."

She said nothing as the door shut behind her. I waited a few minutes, forcing myself not to go after her. Even now, I could still smell her. Feel her. My fingers twitched at the memory of her skin against mine. Shaking my head, I went back to my desk, bringing up the cameras. It took me two seconds to find her.

Adam had left the copy room by the time she got back there. Sydney poked her head around the door, making sure the coast was clear. As soon as she realized she was alone, she slipped inside, back pressing against the door as it closed. Her hand slipped beneath her blouse, the switchblade from last night flashing in the camera.

Curious, I watched her.

The blade popped out before she flicked it closed again. Over and over she did this, taking deep breaths. I watched her chest rise and fall each time, her lips slightly parted and eyes closed. There was something so mesmerizing about her movements. Each flick was controlled as if she'd been doing that her entire life. As if a blade in her hand was the most natural thing in the world rather than pushing papers and fetching reports.

Feeling frustrated, I closed the application. Here I was, stalking my secretary like some insane boss, when I'd never given two shits about them before. There was just something about her that pulled me in, making it hard to think properly. And that was a problem. I shouldn't feel anything toward her. She was just another human. Another secretary that probably wouldn't even last a month.

But there was something about her that I couldn't quite shake.

I had no idea who Sydney truly was, but something told me she wasn't just a secretary.

She wasn't just an ordinary human.

THE LYCAN KING

SYDNEY

I left his office as quickly as I could, making my way back to the copy room. Double-checking to see if Adam was still around, before I slipped inside and shut the door behind me. I was so stupid. There was absolutely no reason for me to hit Adam like that. I'd let my emotions get the better of me and it couldn't happen again.

Feeling anxious, my hand slipped under my blouse, my switchblades familiar weight in my hand. Flicking it open and close in time with my breathing, I tried to calm myself down. Last night's attack had gotten to me more than I thought it had. I believed I had it under control. That I could handle this.

Apparently, I've made my own boss think I'm insane.

Then again... maybe I am fucking insane. Would actually make a lot of sense.

The entire time I was in his office, I felt like there'd been too much tension between us, drawing me closer without me ever realizing it. Before I knew it, I was inches away, our eyes locked, his mouth just...

Nope.

I wasn't going to go there. The last thing I needed was to ruin a mission because I was seduced by the very guy I was looking into. I had to stay focused. I couldn't give my family any reason to second guess my abilities to complete these missions.

Tucking my switchblade back into its sheath, I started working on the reports. It was a mindless task. I already knew there wasn't anything in them that I needed to know. On the business side of things, Noah's company seemed clean enough. If there was anything linking his business to the attacks happening, they weren't in there.

Which meant I was wasting time trying to find the information I really needed.

It was difficult. I had no idea what to look for and it wasn't like it would just pop out with a sign that said 'Noah Solvmane has been ordering the attacks!'. Which meant I would have to take a deeper dive into the company. Maybe start hanging around the staff more to try and see if I can overhear anything at all. There had to be something here. I didn't want to go home empty-handed.

Stacking the reports, I headed back to my desk. At first, nothing seemed off. Then I caught sight of the bright yellow sticky note on the keyboard. Glancing around, I hesitantly picked it up.

We need to meet. Tonight. - Pat

My heart sank as I read the words over and over. I didn't even know how my brother got up here in the first place, or why he wouldn't just text me. But he was always one for dramatics. He liked the suspense. The fear he instilled in others. If he was playing his tricks on me, then he must really be pleased with himself for...something.

Crap.

He couldn't know about the attack last night. I was pretty sure I'd been alone. Otherwise, they would have stepped in. Right? My own family wouldn't just leave me to be shredded to pieces by werewolves. They were EH. They would have stepped in to arrest the supernaturals for their crimes because that's what we did.

Something in my gut told me otherwise.

The rest of the day was spent getting coffee and listening in on other people's conversations, especially the supernaturals. I ran a few errands here and there for Noah, actively staying as far away from him as I could. The times I did have to speak with him, I kept my head down and got out as soon as I could. I didn't know what had happened between us in his office, but it made me nervous.

Finally, at eight, I was ready to go.

I didn't say goodbye to Noah, and didn't bother to ask if he needed anything else. He clearly had my number somehow so he could just text me. I still didn't know how I felt about his admission to looking up my personal number without my consent. Or why he felt the need to do that when he could have just asked.

Nothing about this job was making sense to me.

Grabbing my purse, I headed out as quickly as I could after signing off. I managed to make it to the lobby without anyone else stopping me or trying to get me to do anything more. And as soon as I stepped outside, I took a deep breath trying to release all the built up tension from the day. I had to be at the top of my game when meeting my brother.

He was no one to mess around with.

Arrogant, strategically smart, and a prodigy with any weapon known to man—my brother was my father's golden boy. He had Laurent's cold, calculating brain, his lack of empathy, and his penchant for doing whatever it takes to get the job done. Basically, my father had spent years molding Patrick into his ultimate weapon.

I knew where we were meeting without Patrick even having to say. He hung out around the docks, setting up his own little headquarters that he worked out of. He preferred it that way. Sure, he had his own team and was basically running EH right under our father, but he preferred to keep his distance.

It didn't take me long to get there. I stood outside his warehouse, shivering in the chilly night as I tried to garner up enough courage to go inside. The cameras around the property blinked red, watching my every movement. I had no doubt Patrick was waiting inside for me with that shit-eating grin on his face while he watched me from the cameras.

Like the weirdo he was. I'll never understand why I couldn't have had normal siblings.

Not wanting to give him the satisfaction any longer, I stalked inside. The warehouse was colder, and more desolate though everything was perfectly in order. The open space in the center was mostly filled with training equipment; ropes and bars, weapons, and targets. He'd basically set up his own little shooting range in the place. Computers lined one side, their screens dark now save for the one with the camera feeds on it. The other side was lined with lockers, filled with bullet-proof vests, cases of silver ammo, and his favorite weapons.

He was waiting for me in the center of the room, fists wrapped as he pounded into the speed ball. Sweat glistened along his skin as his dirty blond hair stuck against his forehead. This was typical behavior of my brother. Man didn't know a damn thing about taking it easy. He looked over his shoulder at me, and I spotted the sadistic gleam in his green eyes—the same as mine without the warmth and humanity in them.

Patrick caught the ball between his hands, steadying it. "Took you long enough."

"I had work," I replied dryly. "You know, the mission I'm currently on that you could have put in jeopardy with your little note? How did you even get in?"

He cast me a sideways look, winking. "I have my ways, little sister."

I bit back a retort to that. "Why did you want to meet?"

"We know about your little meet and greet with some Werewolves last night." He started to unwrap the cloth around his hands, glancing up at me. "Seems like you got into a bit of trouble there."

My stomach sank. "You saw me get attacked and you didn't do anything?" Fire ignited in my chest, mixing with pain. "Why were you even there? Were you following me?"

"I was making sure you didn't screw anything up," he replied evenly. "And it's a good thing I was."

"What—" I tried to think. "Why were you even there?"

"Why do you think?"

It took me a second to work that out. There could have been only one reason why my brother would be following me. "Father doesn't trust me, does he?"

Patrick snorted. "That's an understatement. I'm not sure why he gave you this mission. Neither Melissa or I can say we understand it, but he has. But that doesn't mean he believes you can do it, Sydney." He paused for a minute, the edges of his lips twitching. "This is a test. One I'm not so sure you're going to be able to pass."

"Watch me," I snarled. "You have no idea what I'm capable of. We had the same training. The same father. I can do this just as well as any of you."

"Can you?" he asked, mildly amused. I bristled under his scrutiny. "You don't remember much from last night, do you?" He stopped, head tilting to the side. On others, it would seem innocent. With Patrick, I felt like I was being sized up by a mountain lion about to attack.

"I hit my head," I replied shortly. "But I remember enough. I know there were two werewolves and something else came to stop them."

"So you remember your boss turning into a Lycan to save you?"

That threw me off. "What?"

"Fortunately for you, we were about to step in to save your ass," my brother continued, "but then the oddest thing happened. A werewolf like I'd never seen before stepped in before we could, tearing those monsters into pieces. I thought I was going to have to save you from that beast as well... until he shifted back—into your boss."

"I—" I had no idea what to say. I didn't remember that. But I did remember the third werewolf or at least I thought it was.

"Do you know what he is, Sydney?" Patrick's voice dropped as he stalked closer. "He's not a Werewolf, Syd. He's the Lycanthrope. The King of the Shifters. The Lycan is often thought to be a Werewolf, but they are much more. Werewolves can either be human or animal. The Lycan... well, that's a beast that can be both at the same time. A creature bigger, stronger, and faster than any other shifter. A monster that haunts the nightmares of Elite Humanity children... and a man we never knew the identity of until just now.

All because of your little mistake. Which in the end turned out to be helpful."

My mouth parted but no words came out. My mind went blank, unable to process what my brother had just said. Noah couldn't be the Lycan King Elite Humanity had spent decades trying to track down. There was no way he'd been hiding under their noses this entire time. There was no way I'd been working with him and never sensed it.

Patrick stopped a foot away, his face darkening. There was a warning in his gaze, a hint of danger that made my stomach curdle. "You cannot screw this up now. What started out as a simple info-grab has now become so much more. I don't care if you have to sleep with the man, but we need you to get as close as possible."

"Why?" The word came out as nothing but a whisper. It was all I could manage.

"Because he's the boss, kiddo. If we take him down, we rattle the entire supernatural world. We kill him, and Elite Humanity won't ever have to worry about an uprising ever again. That's how the game is played." Patrick shot me a chilling smile that made my heart sink to my stomach. "You take out the king to win the war."

And I was the pawn they wanted to use to do it.

JUMPING TO CONCLUSIONS

NOAH

I couldn't get her out of my mind. It didn't matter what I tried to focus on, my eyes strayed to the cameras on my computer screen, locked onto her desk. She'd been sitting outside my office for the past few hours, working as usual, though more reserved than ever before. At least the paranoia had subsided a little.

And she hadn't attacked any more of my workers... yet.

My fingers pulled at the knot around my throat, slipping along the soft material of my tie. The beast inside me, shifting, was always alert to her presence. Her scent was everywhere. There was no escaping it. No escaping her.

I was so screwed.

She was human. A human that probably didn't know people like me existed—which was for the better. There'd be no way in hell I could ever bring her into this world. Especially not now. Whatever this was, it had to be stopped. But I had a feeling I wouldn't be strong enough.

My eyes caught sight of movement on the cameras. Lawson stepped from the elevator on my floor, tugging at his leather jacket before heading down the hall. Sydney perked up as soon as she saw him coming, sitting up straighter at her desk. Her reaction irked me, my eyes glued to her to see if she reacted in any other way around him. I could see her smile, one that made my heart lurch in my chest before settling into the pit of my stomach.

"Shit."

Lawson pushed through the door, not even bothering to knock. "We've got a problem."

I motioned to the chair across my desk as he shut the door behind him. Sydney wouldn't be able to hear anything through these walls. Not that she'd understand what we were talking about anyway. Whatever Lawson had to say, I knew it was about our little problem.

"EH is back in the city."

Alright. Clearly, it wasn't just a 'little' problem.

"How do you know?" I asked.

"Because we caught sight of your favorite golden boy down around the docks the other night." Lawson studied me, watching for a reaction.

I knew who he was talking about. There was only one golden boy in EH. Laurent's son, Patrick. He'd been molded by Laurent to fit his own image. To be as ruthless, as cold-hearted, as his father was. The kid had serious issues, with arrogance being the least unsettling of them all.

"Because of the attacks?" It was a stupid question, but I was still processing.

"I'm assuming so," Lawson replied, sighing. "If Laurent sent his son here...it can't be good. We need to get a handle on this."

"We have no idea why this is even happening," I snapped. "They know the rules. And only a handful are breaking them."

"It could just be random attacks…" Lawson trailed off when he noticed my face.

"No," I growled, "they aren't. Because that would mean my control is slipping. And it's not."

Lawson's hands shifted up in surrender. "I'm just saying. Maybe this isn't some big conspiracy theory. Maybe times are changing and the sups are feeling more restless."

"Then they'll destroy us all. EH only needs one excuse to continue the crusade they started all those years ago."

"There's another issue." Lawson hesitated, fingers tapping along the arm of his chair.

"Well?" My patience for problems was starting to dwindle.

"We got word that they have someone posted here." He paused, letting his words sink in. "In the company."

Red tinged the edges of my vision. "What?"

"EH has someone in Solv Logistics. I'm not sure what they're looking for. Maybe to see if we have anything to do with these little acts of rebellion but…I thought you should know." Lawson's eyes flicked toward the office door. "You don't think…?"

It took me a few seconds to get what he was suggesting. My fists curled atop my desk. "No."

"Noah—"

"It's not her."

"How do you know?" he shot back.

"Because I know." But the doubt was still there. Clearing my throat, I continued, "We'll start going out each night and running a few patrols. I want your guys in every sector of this city. Try to see who's behind encouraging these attacks and if it's something more than a few errant supernaturals. You and I will stake out EH and try to figure out the snake in our company."

I could tell by the look in his eyes that he already had a suspect, but I wasn't going to encourage that kind of thinking. Sydney was too...innocent.

Not that innocent apparently. Images of her switchblade flashed through my mind. The way she'd had Adam backed against a wall in mere seconds the minute he'd reached for her hand. But it couldn't be her. She was human, sure. But she was also young. Besides, no EH agent would ever allow two werewolves to jump them in some back alleyway.

I caught Lawson's eyes, a warning in my own. "We'll go tonight."

As soon as the sun had dropped behind the skyscrapers, we were out on the streets. Lawson was in his usual attire; a black leather jacket with a matching t-shirt underneath. His jeans were loose with a few holes around his knees. In other words, he was dressed in clothes he wouldn't mind shredding should anything happen.

I was dressed similarly. The gray sweatpants were older than I was, worn but still practical. The dark t-shirt clung to my muscles as we walked down the street, but it wouldn't be too much of a loss in case I needed to shift. We hadn't done patrols in years. Not since the EH left New York City in peace.

Before, we'd mostly done protection routes, making sure Elite Humanity wasn't breaking their own rules they so maliciously enforced on us. As King of the Lycans, I ran these streets to protect everyone; human and supernatural alike. Lawson never argued with me when I ran with them. I think he enjoyed the time we spent together outside of the office.

Tonight felt different, however. Something in the air felt off. I could feel it. My wolf could feel it. Hell, even the humans could feel it. With news traveling around the city of an increase in attacks, the humans weren't as active as they had been before. The streets were emptier, though a few here and there dared challenge the city at night. I couldn't tell if they were brave or stupid.

Or both.

"Where are we headed?" Lawson asked, glancing around. He was on edge tonight.

"The docks. Where you last saw Patrick." I kept moving straight ahead, my focus on one thing and one thing only.

"Are you sure that's smart?" Lawson tugged at his jacket lapel. "We don't want to give them any reason to—"

"They won't do shit."

"Noah..." He trailed off, thinking over his words. "They still don't know your identity. We've managed to at least keep that from them for this long. I don't want to blow your cover over maybe's and if's."

He wasn't wrong, but I was coming to an end I couldn't keep ignoring. Even if it wasn't good that they might know who I was, it didn't matter anymore. In reality, maybe it would be good if they knew. Then maybe they would wake up and fear me like they should.

Shooting him a dark look, I frowned. "If they're sneaking around my company after this many years, then I'm guessing they already suspect who I am."

He fell silent, falling into step beside me. My beast shifted inside me, anxious to be out again. We rarely let our beasts out within the city limits. It was too dangerous, with too many people around. But that didn't stop them from pulling at their tethers every now and then.

Tethers that took years of training to put in place. Some days I wished I had it easy like a typical Werewolf. Perhaps then it would have been easier to maintain control, but being a Lycan, I was far more than just a wolf. I was a rabid beast at times, a dark creature out for blood.

The docks Lawson led me to was just at the edge of Manhattan, secluded in the warehouse district. Here, there were fewer people. Fewer lights. Patrick was smart to choose this as his headquarters if that was the case. If anything went down here, there wouldn't be too many witnesses.

Not that I was expecting anything to happen.

Elite Humanity was very careful to curate the right image. They viewed themselves as the saviors of humanity, protecting the weak from the super-powered. They wouldn't do anything to jeopardize that and make themselves look like the villains.

At least, Laurent wouldn't.

His son was a whole other issue.

A fence lined the outside of the district. Beyond the barbed wire, shipping containers were stacked like a small city, towering over the narrow alleyways they created. I reached out, testing the fence. It was weak, with a few holes along the poles that held it up.

"We stick together," I growled, slipping through one such hole. Lawson said nothing as he followed me in. He knew the drill, and even though he was my brother, I was still in charge.

It was quiet here. Desolate. I could still hear the sounds of the city beyond the barren streets that led to the river. Sirens echoed between the buildings, the muted sounds of cars honking filling the silence in between. The moon hung heavy over the city, its light giving off just enough to make out that which lay in the shadows.

We stalked between the shipping containers, keeping an eye out for anything that didn't belong there. If I were Patrick, I'd stick close to the river. It was an easy backup plan should anything go wrong. But we saw nothing. Heard nothing. I was almost about to give up and head back until I noticed the light on in the warehouse by the river.

It could have been nothing. Probably some night worker watching television on his phone while the dead hours passed by. But I had a feeling it wasn't. Our footsteps were silent as we neared the building, keeping an eye on our surroundings. I wasn't about to be ambushed. Beside me, Lawson's body was tense and ready just in case.

"You boys lost?"

I let out a warning growl, whipping around to my right. A man leaned against one of the containers, arms crossed, though his body was anything but relaxed. Sharp green eyes watched us from the shadows, his hair nearly silver in the moonlight.

"Patrick." I sneered. "You must be Laurent's son."

"And you must be this mysterious King Elite Humanity's been chasing for years." He didn't seem surprised to see me. Apparently, Lawson's intel of them having a leak in our company had been correct. I didn't like being right—about them suspecting who I was—but clearly, I had been.

"I would say it's nice to meet you, but I doubt we both feel that way," I replied evenly. None of us moved. Lawson flashed his canines in warning as Patrick took a step closer.

"You're just the person I hoped to run into tonight, actually," Patrick said, stopping just a few feet away. He seemed unconcerned that he was facing off with two full-grown Lycans. Then again, he had no reason to worry. Not when he was Laurent's son. "A little mouse let me know you'd be out tonight."

My eyes narrowed. "You mean your rat."

Patrick made a tsk tsk with his tongue. "That's unnecessarily rude."

"Whatever you think you'll find, you'll be sorely disappointed."

"Is that why you came looking for me?" Patrick's head tilted to the side, studying us.

"I came to tell you that we have nothing to do with whatever is going on," I replied. "We're trying to figure out why the attacks are happening just as you are."

"We know why the attacks are happening," Patrick snarled, his control slipping. "It seems their King doesn't have as much control as he thinks he does."

My fingers curled at my side. "There's no proof that I'm behind this. Elite Humanity still has its protocols, do they not?"

Patrick's lip curled with irritation. "Fortunately for you. But that won't last long. Our little mouse will find something eventually. And when she does, we'll be ready."

Lawson lunged forward before I could stop him. But Patrick was already gone. Smoke blossomed from where he'd been standing moments ago, curling around our ankles and filling our noses. Coughing, Lawson fell back, wiping the smoke from his eyes.

"That fucking kid." He swore under his breath before glancing over at me. "Now do you believe me? It has to be her, Noah. He said 'she'."

"'She' could mean anyone," I snapped. "You leave the rat to me. I want you to follow him." I nodded to where Patrick had disappeared. "Keep your eyes out on this block. Watch where he goes. We'll find out what they're really up to soon enough."

There was no way I was going to believe that *my secretary*, sweet and scared looking Sydney, was going to be the EH rat. She barely looked like she knew how to keep her composure around me, and it was clear she was jumpy around other men. EH agents were far to trained for something like that.

My brother was going to have to find someone else to accuse.

HIGH ALERT

Sydney

I stopped short as I walked through the front doors of Solv Logistics. Men, I didn't recognize were stationed around the lobby, black pieces looped around their ears. Their black suits looked clean and stiff, much like their demeanor. They studied the small crowd of workers as we filtered through the turnstiles, keeping an eye on us.

"Sydney!"

I turned, greeting Aria as she wiggled her way toward the elevators.

"What's going on?" I asked, nodding toward the men in black.

Aria glanced over her shoulder. "I have no idea. I heard something about a security breach, though." Her large blue eyes met mine, widening slightly, as if we shared a secret.

My stomach dropped at her words. There was no reason to suspect the new security was because of me. And besides, my father would pull me out if Noah figured out who I really was. Laurent might not care what happened to me personally, but he'd definitely care about risking the mission. If I was still here this morning with no message to abort, then that meant Noah hadn't figured out who the breach actually was.

Or at least I hoped that was the case.

Trying to remain calm, I kept my composure and walked with Aria towards the elevators. When the doors opened, a group of us stepped in, and though I knew no one was watching us, I couldn't help but feel that someone was... more importantly they were watching me.

Taking a deep breath, I tried to clear the negativity from my mind. There was no reason to panic just yet. Besides, it's not like I've found anything. Every report, every paper I'd read, had nothing but business deals and shipping notes on it. There was nothing that connected Noah to the attacks, as my father assumed. At least as far as I could tell. The guy—and his business—were clean.

"This is so stupid," Aria muttered. I glanced up, finding another man in a suit slipping into the elevator. He looked straight ahead, shades as black as midnight.

"The glasses are a little overkill," I whispered, trying to lighten the mood.

"Speaking of overkill..." She pulled me closer, looping her arm through mine. "Did I hear you turned Adam down for a date?"

"Is that what he said?" I kept my eyes on the security guy, afraid my face might give something away. At least he hadn't told her the actual truth; that I'd punched him in the face like a psycho. I doubt she'd be talking to me now if he had.

"He said you definitely turned him down. Gave a pretty clear answer, apparently."

Apparently. I bit back a small smile. At the time, it hadn't been funny, but now I couldn't help but picture Adam's face when I'd hit him in the copy room. I also felt sort of bad about it. He hadn't done anything wrong, and I knew I hadn't been in any real danger. I'd let my paranoia get the better of me.

I should probably apologize to the poor guy.

"I'm just not really looking to date anyone right now," I replied.

"Oh?" Aria's eyebrow quirked up. "So it has nothing to do with a super sexy and mysterious boss that happens to work in the office right beside your desk?"

My cheeks burned, and I quickly glanced around to make sure no one else had overheard. "Definitely not," I hissed. "He's the last thing on my mind right now. I just have... a lot going on. Family stuff."

"Whatever you say," Aria replied, looking anything but convinced.

I waved her off as the elevator stopped on her floor. Little by little, the elevator crowd thinned out, including the security guard. He left without a backward glance, but I didn't relax until I finally reached my desk. Slipping out my phone, I sent a quick message to my father. If something came up, I wanted to know about it. And clearly, something had set Noah off to hire more security and, therefore, made my job ten times more difficult. I didn't trust that my father and Elite Humanity would tell me the whole truth, but I expected at least the bare minimum.

After waiting for what seemed like an hour, I still had no response. Deleting the message thread, I sat back in my chair, trying not to panic. I would still be expected to do my job—my first and only mission that wasn't too difficult in the first place. All I needed was information. That was it. And I had it all right at my fingertips.

Rather than focusing on the mounting anxiety, I prepared for the workday. Getting Noah's schedule together took less time than before now that I'd gotten the hang of the system. And at least there weren't any reports to put together today.

Knocking on Noah's door, I waited to be called in for the morning update. When I heard nothing, I hesitated. The clock was ticking, and I knew if I wasn't in there at the exact time he wanted, I'd probably be berated. Then again, it's not like I could have just walked into his office.

Or... could I? I guess it's better to ask for forgiveness than permission.

Nudging it open, I slipped inside. Noah was at his desk, staring intently at his computer screen. His hands were laced in front of his mouth, brow furrowed. For a minute, all I could do was stare. His dark hair wasn't gelled today, soft and curling over his forehead. His dark suit made his gray eyes more intense.

"Sir?" The word tasted weird in my mouth.

Noah's shoulders tensed as his head whipped around. At first, it didn't seem like he'd recognized me. There was a curl to his lip, a ferocity that sent chills down my spine. His gray eyes were like ice, freezing me in place.

But the look was gone as quickly as it had come.

Smoothing his features, Noah cleared his throat. "The morning updates?"

"Y-yes," I replied quietly, finding my voice. "There's only one meeting on the agenda today. For lunch."

"I need you to move it to dinner." His eyes slid away from me as if he couldn't bear to look at me for a moment longer.

"A meeting..."

"For dinner, yes." His words were short and clipped. "At Romano's. Eight o'clock."

Scribbling the information down on the printed schedule sheet, I nodded. I knew Romano's. It was one of the fanciest restaurants in Manhattan and well-known for its spectacular views of the Hudson. "Anything else?"

Noah's eyes darted back to mine, an emotion I couldn't identify flickering amongst the gray. Something about my interactions with him constantly left me breathless. Then again, why wouldn't they? He was absolutely gorgeous and had all the aspects of what I was looking for in a man... what any woman would look for in a man.

Standing there quietly waiting for him to reply, I watched as his eyes slid further down my body, running along my curves until I was left shivering from his cold gaze. Fantasy-based images quickly flashed through my mind I had to force away. As much as part of me wanted to hate him, I couldn't, and that drove me crazy. "What are you doing at eight?"

"Me?" My mouth went dry as I tried to process his question. Why the fuck would he ask me what I'm doing? Taking a moment, Aria's words from earlier echoed through my head.

So it has nothing to do with a super sexy and mysterious boss that happens to work in the office right beside your desk?

Noah waited for my reply, his face unreadable. This was bad. Now that I knew who he was—what he was—I knew spending any more time around him would potentially blow my cover. If he didn't suspect me already. Noah wasn't just any supernatural. He was royalty. From a bloodline my family had been chasing down for hundreds of years.

Paired with the fact Noah clearly suspected something was going on in his company, it would be a horrible idea for me to stick around longer than I had to. I just needed a good excuse. Aria's invitation to grab a drink from before popped up first thing.

"I was going out with—"

"Cancel." His reply was so abrupt, it took me a few minutes to process it.

"I can't just cancel." I had no plans, but he didn't know that. And the fact he expected me to cancel anything outside of my actual work hours was a type of arrogance that made me want to dig my heels in. "Besides, I'm off hours. You can't just demand—"

Noah turned away, looking bored. "Your contract says otherwise."

"What?" I hadn't actually read the papers Mr. Grey had put in front of me. It had never mattered because my employment here was a farce.

"You're to be readily available during and outside of normal working hours due to the position you were hired for," Noah explained, continuing on as if this were a normal conversation about the weather and not about how he basically owned my personal life. "So you will be here, dressed appropriately, at eight."

And just like that he became a complete douchebag all over again.

Heat flared along my cheeks, as I stood staring at him. "Fine, anything else?"

My tone was laced with irritation and I had no doubt he knew that. However, he didn't acknowledge it as he waved a hand toward the door. "You're dismissed."

Gripping my planner and his schedule, I hurried back through the office door. Nothing I said would have mattered. Clearly, I had no say in whether I went to this business dinner or not. Although...it wouldn't technically be a bad thing. With the added security in the building and Noah on high alert, it would be more difficult for me to get any information here. Going with Noah would give me a chance to see more about what he did. If he didn't suspect me and thought I was a normal human who wasn't aware of the existence of supernaturals, then he wouldn't expect me to pick up on anything out of the ordinary.

But I would. I could see past the glamor. I could pick up on any clues that would sound completely normal to anyone else. I'd been trained and groomed for this. To be aware of my surroundings and learn everything I could about the supernaturals.

If this meeting was more than just a business meeting, if there was more to it than simply talking shop, I'd be there to hear it all. And it might just give me the in I'd need to complete this mission and prove myself to everyone. Not that I cared about proving my family wrong, but it would be pretty damn nice to see the looks on my siblings' faces when they realized I hadn't totally screwed this up.

My brother's comment hit me like a brick wall, knocking my sense of accomplishment to the ground.

I don't care if you have to sleep with the man, but we need you to get as close as possible.

Fire licked at my core, heat flaring between my thighs. The idea didn't sound as disgusting as it should have and that's what worried me. If I didn't get the information I needed from this dinner, if I couldn't fulfill my mission tonight, then clearly I'd have to step up my game.

Even if I had to sleep with a monster.

I just hoped it wouldn't turn around and bite me in the ass later.

DINNER & SURPRISES

Sydney

By eight, I was waiting out on the front steps of Solv Logistics. I'd almost considered not showing up just to spite Noah, but I figured that would do more harm than good for my job and mission. I'd grown up knowing there would be things I had to do that I didn't want to do when it came to my family's job duties.

Going out with my monstrous and slightly obnoxious boss was just one example.

The night quickly grew chilly, raising goosebumps along my bare arms. I'd had to dig in my closet for something presentable to wear. The emerald green dress was a bit tight, hugging every curve, but still somewhat comfortable. I'd opted for heels, just because I knew the restaurant we were going to was way too fancy for even flats. Overall, I knew I looked good.

"Is that what you're wearing?"

Turning, I found Noah at the top of the steps. He wore the same suit he'd had on all day, though he'd gelled his hair back since I'd last seen him. Those silver eyes ran down my body, lip curling slightly. I was used to the cold looks and brush-offs but this was different.

For the first time since I met him, I felt as if he were really seeing me.

And, clearly, he didn't like what he saw.

"Is there a problem?" I asked, glancing down at my attire and then back to him with a raised brow. "Because, if there is, I really don't need to go. I had other plans."

His gaze swept up to meet mine. "No, you didn't," he replied stiffly. "And that dress is a bit...tight. Do you not own something more appropriate?"

Oh for the love of...

"Appropriate?" I scoffed. "This isn't even a low-cut dress." And it wasn't. The sweetheart neckline was well above my cleavage line, hiding everything that mattered, while the skirt fell halfway down my thighs. Sure, it might have been a little snug, but it wasn't as if I was exposing myself to everyone on the street.

Noah's jaw flexed, his fingers curling at his side. Before he could say anything, I heard the sound of tires pulling up to the building. Noah's lips thinned as he brushed past me, heading for the sleek town car sitting idle at the side of the road. It was clear he wasn't going to say anything else on the matter, and it was best he didn't.

Turning towards the car, I was slightly surprised by what Noah was doing. He stood at the back door to the car, waiting for me with the door wide open for me to slide in.

Interesting... perhaps he is a gentleman after all.

I made myself as small as possible as I ducked beneath his arm, scooting over to the far side of the car. He wasted no time as he slid in behind me, taking up more space than he had any right to. Clenching my thighs together, I tried to avoid touching him, though he didn't make it easy.

"Who are we meeting with tonight?" I asked, tugging the hem of my skirt over my knees. It had ridden up slightly, making me even more self-conscious after his little comment minutes prior.

"Clients."

Well, no shit. As if that told me anything. I handled his schedule. I knew they were clients. I just didn't know who they were or who they worked for. I didn't even know if they'd be human or something else, though I hoped it was the latter. At least then I might learn something useful and get my siblings off my back.

"Any particular client or...?" I let my words trail off, waiting for him to take the bait.

"High-end clients."

This guy was seriously aggravating. Of course, he couldn't make my job easy. That would be too nice of him. And Noah Solvmane didn't seem to do nice.

"Alright then," I replied in irritation. I really didn't have much else to say. If he wanted to be annoyingly mysterious, then fine. I'd find out when we got there anyway.

We sat in dead silence as the car pulled away from the company's front steps, weaving between late New York City traffic. The restaurant wasn't too far away, but knowing the driving around here, I knew it would take us at least forty-five minutes. Which seemed like torture considering my boss was sitting ice-cold beside me and glaring out the window.

What's got his panties in a bunch?

I stayed quiet, not wanting to antagonize the actual beast in the car. There had to have been a reason why he'd invited me tonight—some sort of plan I didn't know about. My brain flipped through my most recent actions the past few days, wondering if I really had let something slip. It couldn't be a coincidence that he'd hired more security guards at the office and invited me out to some random dinner meeting.

He didn't know, did he?

By the time the car finally pulled up to Romano's, I was sweating. It was one thing to see him at work every day and entirely another to actually go out with him to some fancy restaurant. I didn't think this was a trap—it was too public. If Noah suspected anything about me, I doubted he'd be taking me out to dinner.

Though when he climbed out of the car in silence, I began to worry again.

Noah waited for me to slip out of the car, but he didn't seem too happy about it. It was hard not to catalog his every movement, every facial expression. The slight downward tip of his brows, the twitch of his lip as I nearly stumbled on the sidewalk. He was acting colder than ever before. More distant.

I didn't know what to make of it.

"Reservation?" The hostess beamed at Noah, her eyes traveling down his body like he was some enormous buffet and she was starved.

"Noah Solvmane." He barely glanced at her, eyes scanning the open dining area beyond the hostess stand. "Party of four."

She checked her tablet, looking slightly disappointed. "You can follow me. Your other guests haven't arrived just yet."

"Thank you."

Following her to our table, she weaved around couples enjoying their food and the odd waitress carrying a tray until we arrived at a table in the very back. I couldn't help but notice how reclusive it was. The table was tucked into a small corner by the floor-to-ceiling windows, overlooking the city, far enough away from the other patrons so as to not be overheard. Mentally, I clocked the various possible exits.

Just in case.

Tentatively, I took a seat beside Noah, still unsure why I was even here. Was I supposed to bring a notebook? Take notes? Sit here and look pretty? I eyed Noah as if his icy demeanor would give me a damn clue, but he was about as walled up as a medieval fortress.

"Staring is considered rude," Noah muttered, perusing the wine menu.

"Why am I here?"

"Because I want you here." He seemed completely unbothered by my tone of voice. But I'd be lying if I didn't admit that my heart jumped just a bit when he said he wanted me here.

"That doesn't explain anything," I argued, arms crossing over my chest. I felt like a petulant child, but he was really getting on my nerves.

Noah sighed, setting the menu aside. "Because I could use the help to diffuse a difficult situation. And you're... smart." The last bit of his statement made it seem as if he was reluctant to admit that bit of information, and something about it I found amusing.

"What sort of difficult situation?" I asked, deciding to press a few more buttons.

"You have some nerve, Solvmane." A heavy-set man stalked toward our table. Red bloomed across his round cheeks, his forehead beading with sweat. The suit he wore barely fit him, nearly as tight as my dress. The buttons were hanging on for dear life. Behind him, a frailer woman trailed behind him, glancing around the restaurant as other patrons turned their way. To my disappointment, they were both human.

"Sydney, this is Mr. And Mrs. Anderson," Noah straightened, a sense of calm washing over him. "This is my assistant, Sydney."

"I don't give a damn who that is," Mr. Anderson spluttered. He towered over Noah, using his full weight to appear more intimidating, but he was failing. Miserably might I add. "You don't just get to nearly ruin my business and then demand a meeting as if I have no choice in the matter."

"Sit down, Arnold," Noah replied, sounding slightly bored. Almost as if he had clearly expected this. "I want to discuss the future of your business."

"Why in the—"

"Sit."

Mr. Anderson muttered something beneath his breath I didn't quite catch, but I assumed it wasn't appropriate for this place. He did as he was told, however. I don't think anyone could refuse Noah—not when he spoke like that. His wife even followed, demurely sitting beside him. An embarrassed smile coursing her lips as she met my gaze.

"Now," Noah leaned forward, elbows resting on the table, "your transportation company was already going under—"

"And your buyout nearly ruined us," Mr. Anderson growled.

"My buyout might just be the very thing to save you." Noah caught his gaze and held it for a beat before continuing. "Solv Logistics focuses mainly on international transportation of goods between multiple Fortune 500 businesses, as you know. However, I'd like to focus more on our local companies. Specifically in the poorer areas of New York City."

"And why would I do that?" Anderson snorted. "There's no money in that."

"There will be," Noah countered. "I'll pay your company a hefty fee to work on the transportation of goods for local businesses. Many of them can't afford to get their supplies due to the shortages recently. I want to rectify that."

I eyed Noah warily.

"And what's in it for you?" Anderson asked cautiously.

Noah shrugged, leaning back in his chair. "Tax write-offs. Charity. Whatever I need it to be."

Anderson seemed to struggle with that answer as if it were completely unexpected. Which it was. Even I couldn't fathom why Noah would do something like this. His company was one of the most well-established logistics companies in the U.S. He didn't need to do any sort of charity, and I'm pretty sure he didn't need the tax write-offs either.

And he definitely didn't seem like the charitable type.

Anderson's eyes narrowed. "I don't understand."

I'm right there with you on that one, buddy. I internally thought as I lifted my water glass to my lips trying to keep myself out of the hot mess this man was obviously in.

"I'll be reaching out to local businesses throughout New York City that usually ships their supplies in from out of state. Based on their needs, I'll need to expand my transportation department to cover those orders. That's where you come in. We do this merger, and not only will your business be saved, but you'll be able to continue the...lifestyle, I know you enjoy." Noah's gaze slid down Anderson's well-endowed body. "It's a win-win for both of us."

"How much are we talking about?" Anderson asked finally. He seemed more relaxed, though the red flush was still present. Noah would never be the type of person to make someone feel completely comfortable.

"More than what you were making before," Noah assured. "I'll have Sydney and Mr. Grey go over the specifics this week."

Anderson sniffed, glancing at his wife. I caught the slight nod she gave him, though it was nearly imperceptible. "I'm not sure if I should trust you, but I'm not entirely opposed to this idea. But I'll want a detailed report on how, exactly, this will work."

Noah grinned—the first real smile I'd seen on his face since I met him. "Wonderful. Now, what wine do you prefer?"

I still had no idea why Noah bothered to bring me along. Noah and Mr. Anderson avoided discussing the details of their new deal over dinner, which was a bummer. I had really been hoping to learn something useful. Even though I doubted that would happen. For the first half, I was attentive, trying to catch anything that might give me more insight to what, exactly, Noah had to do with the supernatural attacks. Yet I quickly realized there was no way he'd bring that up with a human.

So, I sat there confused.

Elite Humanity must have somehow suspected what Noah was from the start. If he was the King of the Lycans, he'd certainly be a suspect if any rebellions popped up across the United States. It made sense. The vampires were too solitary to have any sort of King or Queen to lead them. The Faeries had their own government system and loved to play tricks, but they left humans alone for the most part. Shifters tended to stay with their own breed, and though they had pack leaders, we always knew that it was something far greater than the normal governing systems. Out of all the supernaturals we had intel on, the Lycans were the one species we barely knew anything about.

Lycan's were rare. They were more closely related to Werewolves but they weren't. They were monsters born from the shadows, said to have once guarded the gates of hell… or something like that. Thoughts of an old bedtime story my mother once told me circled through my mind, and though I didn't remember all of it, I remembered one distinct line.

From the shadows came the beast, his eyes sought upon the human feast. Though the dangers rang high and clear, only one could tame him here.

It was weird to still remember such a thing, but sitting here now I found it even stranger to compare Noah to the beast from those stories. He seemed so normal and even though I was slightly unsure about him, I definitely didn't see him as a murderous beast.

And definitely not one to start a rebellion.

"Sydney?" Noah's voice pulled me from my thoughts like a splash of icy water.

"Sorry?" I realized pretty quickly that someone had clearly asked me a question. The entire table stared at me, waiting for my answer.

"Have you always lived in New York City?" Mrs. Anderson repeated slowly. There was no judgment in her voice as she slipped me a soft smile.

"No," I replied quickly, trying to gauge how much information I should give away. There'd been a small background briefing when I'd first gone undercover, but I couldn't remember every single detail listed in the folder I'd shredded. "I moved around a bit growing up, and just recently finished college out in California."

"Really? Where did you move around as a child?" Mrs. Anderson pressed. I wanted to like her, but this was starting to feel more like an interrogation. Especially with Noah's eyes locked on me, studying my every breath like a predator.

"Around," I said vaguely.

"On your resume, it said you were in Louisiana for a bit," Noah offered.

I glanced at him in surprise. I didn't even think he'd look over the fake resume I'd handed in when I'd applied let alone remember any details from it.

"I was. For a bit."

"For what?" Mr. Anderson leaned against the table, looking interested. "I've been to New Orleans a few times. Great place. Great food."

"I was there for...school." It wasn't entirely a lie. I'd trained down there out in the middle of the swamps. The perfect place to find supernaturals in hiding.

"Undergraduate?"

"Sure."

Noah's eyes narrowed at my response.

"I mean, yes. I studied business." That was on my resume. I knew it was.

"I thought you studied business in California?" Noah replied casually, lifting his wine glass to his lips. His eyes watched me over the rim.

"I did both." Shifting nervously, I avoided his gaze. "Switched schools. On my resume, I just put the school I'd graduated from."

"Of course." I couldn't read the tone in his voice.

"Would you like another bottle?" A server stopped by our table, glancing around earnestly.

"I believe we're done for the night," Noah said, finishing off his glass. Mr. Anderson looked a little put-out, eyeing the empty bottle on the table. "I'll take the check."

"Certainly." The server disappeared, leaving us to ourselves once again.

"You really don't need to cover this," Mr. Anderson started.

Noah waved him away. "Consider this a start to our new partnership."

Noah and I were once again left alone together, and I couldn't help but wish that Mr. Anderson and his wife would come back. Ever since Mrs. Anderson decided to play twenty-one questions with me, Noah was eyeing me with a suspicious glance that made me nervous. "It's been wonderful, but I think I'll be heading home."

Turning on my heel, I attempted to walk away. I wanted to get as far away from him as I could. A firm grasp on my arm stopped me in my tracks and Noah stepped into my view. I couldn't help but let a heavy sigh escape me.

"I'll take you home. Get in the car."

" No," I scoffed trying to smile as sweetly as I could. "I appreciate that, but I think I'll take a cab."

"I wasn't asking. Now get in the car." Tugging me behind him, I realized there was no way out of this. Pulling my arm from his grasp, he stared at me with dark, dangerous eyes. "If you're going to force me to get a ride from you, don't manhandle me."

"Manhandle you?" He smirked, staring at me with amusement. "If I wanted to manhandle you, I would—and I promise you wouldn't complain."

Fuck... why did his sarcastic comment sound sexier than it should have?

SUBMITTING TO A KING

SYDNEY

Noah Solvmane was a lot of things, but amusing wasn't a quality I would have included. He sat next to me in the back seat of the sedan, staring at me with a smirk on his face that completely caught me off guard. I didn't understand what his problem was, but something about the way he was looking at me seemed more amusing than anything.

Glancing out the windows, I tried to distract myself from the irritating man next to me—no matter how amazing his cologne was. I realized we were heading in the direction of my apartment, which sent red flags raising in the air.

"How do you know where I live?" I snapped, harsher than I needed to as my head jerked in his direction.

Noah was silent for a beat, as his smile fell and an emotion I couldn't decipher flashed in his eyes. "Your resume, of course."

Of course. Because he wasn't going to admit that he was the one who had saved me that night.

"Right." Heat flooded my cheeks. He didn't know I knew. And now I had just made myself look stupidly paranoid. Though I kind of was.

"Worried about something?"

Narrowing my gaze, I scoffed, "no... do I need to be?"

A spark of frustration lit in my chest. I was tired of his games. He didn't need me to come along to this dinner tonight. He'd handled everything perfectly fine on his own and hadn't even asked me to take notes. With the added security at the office, and from what my brother has told me, Noah Solvmane knew what he was doing.

He had to know what I was.

There was no other reason for all of this.

The drive to my apartment was deadly quiet. My nails cut into my thighs, leaving crescent-shaped marks along my skin. Noah sat like stone beside me the rest of the way, his gaze locked on the view outside the window. It didn't even look like he was breathing, let alone alive. Like one of those Greek marble statues carved to perfection.

As the car pulled up to my house, I waited for him to get out before I slid across the seat. The moment that the fresh air hit my lungs a sigh of relief washed over me knowing that I was almost out of danger. I had expected him to be excited about getting rid of me. To jump back into the sedan again and peel off down the road, but that didn't happen.

The back door slammed shut, the car engine going silent.

"What are you doing?" I asked, panic rising.

"Walking you inside." Noah shot me a sharp look. "Is that a problem?" The challenge in his voice made my stomach drop.

"There's really no need," I replied quickly, hoping to God he'd take the hint.

"It's New York City. At night." As if that wasn't obvious.

Fuck, he isn't going to let this go.

He followed me inside, clearly oblivious to my not-so-subtle attempts at ditching him. I could feel his presence at my back like a physical thing, pressing against my skin until I felt as if I was burning alive. The ride up to the top floor sucked the air from my lungs, my stomach twisting into knots.

As soon as the doors were opened, Noah stepped out, waiting as I fumbled for my keys. It took me three tries to get that damn door open.

"Why do you have so many locks?" Noah asked. There was no suspicion in his voice. No curiosity. He sounded like he already knew the answer.

"Just... paranoid, I guess." Because that wasn't too far off from the truth. I opened the door, blocking the entrance with my body. "Well, thank you for the escort home. I think I'm good now."

"Are you?" Noah's eyes dragged along my body. His rough voice and the steel burning in his eyes set me ablaze in a way I couldn't describe. My heart flipped upside down, the last of my breath stolen from my lungs. "You seem... tense."

He was playing mind games. I knew it. He knew I knew it. I hadn't realized until just then what he was doing.

And that ticked me off.

"I don't need you to babysit me," I snapped. "I'm perfectly capable of getting home on my own."

He moved so fast I barely clocked it.

Rough, callused fingers slipped down my bare arms, tracing the goosebumps that rose to meet his touch. His fingertips grazed over my shoulders and along my collarbone. The sensation he created in me caused my breath to hitch before I remembered exactly what he was doing. He was playing with me, and he was enjoying it.

"You seemed jumpy tonight."

My nails dug into his wrists before I could stop them. Something about him grounded me; the breath flooding into my lungs again as soon as he touched me. "Maybe because my boss followed me to my apartment."

His head tilted, silver eyes catching mine. "Is that so."

It wasn't a question, and I had no answer, even if it was. As he leaned forward, my breath caught in my throat.

Noah reached behind me, opening the door. Before my mind could process what was happening, he had me inside my apartment, my back pressed against the wall. His touch skimmed the outside of my arms, rough palms tracing along my skin, skimming beneath my breasts. I froze, a small part of my brain screaming at me to stop him.

God, I should have.

Blisteringly hot, I felt each electric spark of his touch ripple through me like lightning striking through my core. His thumb brushed over the center of my breast, through the fabric of my dress, a jolt of pleasure rushed between my thighs.

"Why are you here, Sydney?" Noah growled, his breath hot against my ear.

"I'm your secretary." It came out barely as a whisper.

"No." The word cut through the air, harsh and angry. "What are you really doing here?"

Steeling myself, I glared up at him. "Working."

His jaw flexed, frustration clear in his eyes. But there was something else.

A want.

A need.

It was that look that finally broke the dam.

His lips crashed against mine, a fiery blaze that was all-consuming. His hand slid back to my breast, the other dipping down the center of my stomach. I could feel him gripping the edge of my dress before it was yanked over my hips, my body jerking with the motion. I gasped against his mouth when the heat of his palm cupped my center, unable to hold back a moan.

I didn't understand this. Couldn't process what was happening. All I knew was that I didn't want it to stop. A fire lit in my chest, burning through me.

My nails raked down his arm, the padding of his suit limiting the damage I could do. A growl rumbled through my chest, surprising me. He was... frustrating. Always watching me with those silver eyes. Hot one minute before icing me out the next. I didn't know what this meant.

But at that point, I didn't really care.

"That's right, baby girl," Noah murmured. His lips dragged down my neck, his teeth grazing my skin. "Get nice and wet for me."

Oh, God.

One finger traced the slick wetness through my underwear, teasing me. Toying with me. I whimpered as he yanked my panties to the side, working a finger into me, gathering the wetness against my clit. The pace of his finger increased as I bit onto his shoulder to keep myself from screaming out in pleasure.

Pleasure he was creating. It wasn't like anything I had ever felt before.

Breath hissed between his lips as he placed one hand upon my throat, pulling me away from his shoulders, only to take my breath away with a bruising kiss more wild than anything I had ever experienced. A moan escaped me when he finally released me, only to gasp as he spun me around, pinning me to the wall once more. Staggering forward, I braced myself against the wall to keep myself upright. I could feel how hard he was, how badly he wanted me, through his slacks. The hard length of him pressed against my ass, grinding into me.

"God, Sydney…" His hand skimmed over the firm round plump of my backside, a roughness to his movements that left me shivering. "I need to taste you."

Of all the things he could have said, those words were my undoing.

I forced myself back around, catching his mouth with mine. My hands tore at his suit, yanking the jacket from his shoulders. And he let me. I knew he could stop me if he wanted to. Knew he could overpower me and take whatever it was he was after. And that thought alone unleashed something in me I didn't even know I had.

He wasn't gentle. He wasn't kind. His touch bruised me where he gripped my arms, hauling my legs around his waist. His teeth raked against my neck, breathing life into the fire at my core. I didn't realize he'd headed into my bedroom until I was tossed down onto the bed. I didn't even have the patience to play that little game, to ask how he knew where I slept.

All I wanted was him. Right then. Right there.

A ripping sound tore through the air, my mind barely processing his movements as my dress landed in a pile on my floor. His eyes traced the curves of my body before he gripped my ankles, yanking me to the edge of the bed. A moan escaping my lips as his fingers thrusted back inside me, the wet sounds of my desire echoing around my room.

"I want you to cum for me," Noah growled. "Like the good little secretary you are."

His words alone were enough to get me off. Hearing them come from his mouth made me feel dirty. Sexy. Desired. And when his thumb circled my clit, all I could do was let the pleasure consume me. My body jerked beneath his touch, waves of electricity jolting through my body.

"Oh fuck, Noah." His name on my lips seemed to unleash everything he'd been holding back. Because the moment they left my mouth, something far more primal escaped him.

I heard the soft clicking of his belt coming undone, the swish of his slacks hitting the floor. But I didn't care. My hands were already tugging at the buttons of his shirt, yanking the fabric away from his broad, hard chest. His skin burned against my palms as I traced the hard edges of his shoulders.

His fingers receded, leaving me shaking on the bed. But there wasn't enough time to regroup, to think this through. I gasped as he entered me, my back arching to accommodate him. His body pressed down against mine, holding me in place. In one smooth motion, my hands were captured, jerked above my head as he held me down.

Each stroke sent fissures of pleasure down my spine, my mind going completely blank as he took me so completely. I'd never felt anything like it, my body reacting to each deep stroke until there was nothing but him. One hand held my hands against the mattress, the other snaking between our bodies. I didn't know what he was planning until it was too late.

His thumb brushed against my clit, his thrusts deepening.
And I came completely undone.

HESITATION OF THE HEART

NOAH

I hadn't meant for it to go that far. In fact, I hadn't meant for any of that to ever happen. It shouldn't have happened. And yet, here I was, watching Sydney's chest rise and fall with each soft breath as I lay beside her. As if this was actually something.

But it wasn't.

My beast snarled as I slid from the bed carefully, but I ignored him. There was no reason for him to feel this way. For him to want her so much.

Though as I thought that through, I couldn't help but wonder if there was something more to her than just what I knew. My beast had been attracted to her from the moment I laid eyes on her, not to mention the feeling of possessive obsession I felt from the creature.

It was almost as if she was...

The thought died almost as immediately as it begun. There was no way I would even consider going down that road, not to mention, she was human. That on its own wasn't possible. A heavy breath escaped me as I looked over my shoulder at her once more before standing in search of my clothes.

Across the room, on the floor, laid parts of my suit, looking more rumpled than ever, which further showed how primal our entire interaction had been. Soft sounds from behind caused me to halt in my steps as I looked at her once more.

Sydney stirred softly, her body rolling over before going still again. If I was going to leave before she woke, I needed to do it now, and quietly I dressed in what I could find. She rolled over, red hair splayed over the pillow like wildfire, making me stop once more. I wanted more than anything to lay naked beside her again, to wrap my fist within those red locks as I entered her over and over.

Shaking my head, I locked those thoughts away just as quickly as they had come. This feeling of needing her, wanting her, it shouldn't be there. I shouldn't want to have anything to do with her, especially if she had anything to do with that prick of an EH agent's threat.

Someone had infiltrated my company. Someone was spying on me for Elite Humanity.

As I stepped from her bedroom, my eyes scanned her apartment. The last time I'd been here, I hadn't done much. It had never crossed my mind to go through her living space. But now...

I needed to know the truth...

I wander around the living room, fingers trailing along the spines of the books lined up against the walls, along the back of the couch. At a first glance, nothing seemed amiss. Everything looked as it should in a normal human apartment. A blinking light by the door caught my attention—something I hadn't noticed last night.

A security pad—newly added—had been installed by the frame. Its light blinked red, the numbers beneath it in black. I glanced at the locks on her door, noticing one that had been broken and never fixed. My eyes narrowed.

Not so normal.

Turning away from the door, I went around the island counter, seeing if there was anything else I'd missed. But there was nothing. No smell of silver bullets, no weapons that I could sense. The place was clean minus the blade she'd had on her that night she was attacked. It was in her purse that had been tossed to the floor last night.

This is ridiculous... I'm being fucking paranoid.

Forcing myself to abandon this half-assed investigation, I slipped out the door before I made an even bigger fool of myself. I could feel the beast inside me straining to go back to that bedroom, clawing from inside me as I shut the door. I knew why he was acting this way. I'd known since the moment I'd first met her.

I'd just been trying to ignore it—she was my mate. A second chance one.

Enough! We can't replace our mate with another.

My thoughts were sent directly to my beast, who growled in anger at my refusal to accept Sydney as anything other than my secretary. But last night was the first time I'd been with someone since Roya. The first and only person I had touched since her passing. It felt like a betrayal, no matter how much I enjoyed it. I felt like I'd done something I shouldn't have.

Each step that took me further and further from her front door was physically painful. The flashbacks of last night ran through my mind. The way her body pressed against mine, her parted swollen lips moaning for more as her back arched and her eyes rolled back from the pleasure I created in her. Even the way she begged for me to keep fucking her. I wanted all of it. To see and feel all of it all the time, but I knew that wasn't possible.

In the end, the only distraction from those agonizing thoughts was the sound of my phone going off as soon as I stepped outside her building.

"Lawson?"

"There was another attack last night. A woman drained out in a back alley."

"Vampire," I muttered. "Did EH already pick that up?"

"Not from what I can tell," Lawson replied. "We've been tracking him since last night but haven't had any openings to nab him. He's barricaded himself in one of the old subway tunnels."

"You're trying to get to him before EH." It wasn't a question. It was actually a pretty smart plan for Lawson.

"That's the goal. Not sure when they'll swoop in here, though. Might need some backup."

"If EH shows up, I want you out of there," I ordered. "We don't need a run-in with them right now. Not until we figure this out."

Lawson scoffed through the phone. "Well, we won't be able to figure this out if we can't question the damn vamp. We need to know why he broke the rules. If this was just a one-time thing or…"

"Or if something bigger is going on," I finished for him.

"Like you said."

So now he wanted to believe me. "Just don't do anything stupid," I replied.

"I'll keep it clean. No worries."

"Lawson, I mean it."

He picked up on the hard-edged warning in my voice. "I know, Noah. Don't worry." He ended the call before I could say anything else.

I had half a mind to call him back, but dialed my driver instead. If Lawson wanted to test EH in order to get answers, I knew I wouldn't be able to stop him. I might have been the King of the Lycans, but he was my brother. And I knew there would be no getting through to him once he'd set his mind on something. Stubbornness ran in the family, unfortunately. All I could do was wait and make sure he didn't kill himself or my men.

Besides, I had another thing to worry about.

A worry with emerald eyes and hair like fire.

I had no idea what I was supposed to do here. Sydney was human—that was clearly obvious. And her little slip-up last night at dinner about where she'd been living previously had me believing there was more to her than I'd originally thought. Not to mention, no innocent human would carry around a blade like that. It had been perfectly crafted, not something just bought in a store.

The more I began putting all the pieces together, the more I knew I needed to get to the bottom of who she was, and what I was going to do about her. If she was EH, would I be able to walk away from her forever? Would I be able to kill her if she came after me?

There was so much I really needed to consider, and on top of that, I was worried for Lawson who, though I knew could take care of himself, was walking into a potentially very dangerous situation. I could almost hear his reprimand now if he found out I had slept with Sydney. He was so adamant that she was the spy, that she was the EH insider.

Ignoring my internal dilemma, I brought myself back to the present as my driver pulled up to the curb. It didn't matter how I felt about her. She was human. As the King, I couldn't afford to bring her into my world even if there wasn't anything off about her. She wouldn't survive a day being my mate. That was the only thing I was sure of.

She would make me weak. Vulnerable. At least with Roya, I knew she could protect herself. That she was like me. But Sydney? Being a human meant she was more of a risk than an investment. Being with her would cause more problems than I needed right now. Not to mention I would completely lose hold on my kingdom if the supernatural world found out I was mated to someone with ties to EH—if she was.

The best thing for me to do is just to let her be. To ignore her.

But I didn't want that.

My phone screen switched on, the messaging app already pulled up. Her name sat at the top, taunting me. I wanted an excuse to speak with her again, and I could have had I just stayed at her apartment. But I needed to do it on my own terms. Somewhere I knew wouldn't be bugged, and a place I knew was safe. Letting my fingers dance across the keypad, I sent her a message asking her to come to my address to discuss a client contract.

It was a complete lie, but right now, I needed an excuse to get her alone again. It was still the wee hours of Saturday morning and though the day was young, I was glad to be heading home. I needed time to really think things over. To dive deep into the information I knew, to ensure I was prepared for when she arrived.

Though I had a feeling that seeing her again was only going to end the way it had tonight.

That fiery red vixen did shit to my soul I would never be able to understand.

One thing for sure though, I was addicted.

And if I wasn't careful, it would be my downfall.

BROTHERLY AFFECTION

SYDNEY

By the time I woke up, I knew he was gone. The whole night almost seemed like a surreal dream. For a minute, I almost thought it was—that I'd just made up the entire thing in my head. But the soft remnants of pleasure still curling through my body said otherwise.

Jolting upright, I ran my fingers through my hair, the tangles catching at the ends. There was no way last night had happened. No, damn way. It had been stupid and irrational, no matter what advice my brother gave. Because I was pretty sure that, when he'd told me to sleep with Noah, he meant at his house so I could sneak around after. Not screw him in my house where I couldn't get any information.

I'd been so damn stupid.

The space beside me was still warm, which meant Noah had just left. Not that I cared. I shouldn't care. He was my mission and nothing more. He shouldn't matter even if he wasn't a potential suspect for Elite Humanity because he was a Lycan. And not just any Lycan, but the fucking Lycan King.

A monster.

A predator.

A nightmare.

And yet...

The entire time I've worked for him, and been around him, I'd never once felt scared of him. Paranoid, yes. But frightened? Never. Noah wasn't the monster I'd imagined him to be. Wasn't even close.

Everything about him was controlled and contained. Yet beneath all that, I could still sense the primal rage beneath his skin. There was a whole other side of him I hadn't seen before. Last night he'd seemed more... human.

Nope.

I stopped myself from going down that road. Noah Solvmane wasn't human. That was the whole reason why I was here in the first place. Elite Humanity had suspected his company had something to do with the recent attacks, though they might not have known what Noah was just yet. Now that they knew who he was, it made everything that much more complicated.

With attacks on the rise, and a potential rebellion on our hands, I couldn't deny that Noah might have something to do with all of it. He was the King after all. The fucking appointed leader of the supernaturals. He had the power to control supernaturals, at least to some extent. I just wasn't exactly sure how far his power extended, but I knew it had to be vast. His company alone could attest to that. His influence was obvious even in the human world.

Swinging my feet over the edge of the bed, I noticed a few notifications on my phone screen. Without even looking, I knew who they were from. My brother's name was like a warning flare, glaring up at me. I didn't know what the message said just yet, but I knew it couldn't be good.

So you took my advice. Hope it was worth it.

My heart dropped as I read his words, thumbs frozen over the screen. He hadn't been kidding when he said they'd be watching me to make sure I wouldn't screw up. But to know that he knew what I'd done seemed like an invasion of privacy. I wasn't even safe in my own apartment.

I didn't regret what I'd done. My brother would never understand, nor would my sister, but they'd been trained differently than I had. They'd been old enough to remember our mother. Old enough to remember how she died. When they'd found her body, they knew exactly what kind of monster had taken their mother from them.

A monster like Noah.

I should despise him. I should fear him.

I didn't.

And I didn't know if that made me brave or just plain stupid.

I clicked out of my brother's message, going to the one from my father. His was short but to the point.

Another attack last night. We need intel.

My stomach churned at the thought of another life taken. I wondered which type of supernatural had done it this time. If it was a Vampire or a Werewolf... was Noah even aware of these attacks? He had to be. Being King meant something, right?

If there were deaths in his territory, then he'd have to know about it.

Which meant he probably had information about them somewhere. And, so far, there wasn't anything at his company. Which meant that anything related to his position as the Lycan leader would have to be at his house. But there was no way I'd probably ever get invited there. Noah seemed too private to allow his secretary into his personal home, even if he had slept with her.

I needed to figure out a way in.

A banging sounded at my front door, causing me to flinch. Snatching shorts from a nearby chair and a loose tee from my dresser drawers, I tugged them on as I stumbled out into the living room.

"Coming!" I yelled as the banging continued, shaking the new locks I'd had installed.

At least I knew they worked.

"Sydney, I know you're in there." My brother's familiar voice sounded half amused and half annoyed. And that never boded well for me. Every part of me wanted to tell him to fuck off, but I knew he wouldn't leave that easily. In fact, it would only make things worse if I did.

My fingers flew across the number pad of the new lock until the light turned green. There was a soft thump of the door unlocking but before I could reach for the handle, my brother was already shoving it open. He didn't bother to greet me, didn't bother to even apologize for shoving me to the side as he stormed in.

"So how was it?" Patrick sneered, leaning against my couch with his arms crossed as he waited for my answer. I knew what he wanted to hear, but I didn't care. There was no way I was going to share my sex life with him. He suggested that this happen so he just had to accept that it did.

"Why are you here?" I finally asked, closing the door before leaning up against it.

"I wanted to see if you'd like to go hunting with us tonight or if you were too busy with your new distraction." Disgust flickered across his eyes, the tone of his voice hard to ignore.

"He's not a distraction," I snapped. "You told me to get close to him." Actually, he'd definitely told me to sleep with him. But that was Patrick. Always a pain in my ass.

Patrick snorted. "I just didn't expect you to actually listen to me."

"What are you hunting?" I asked warily, knowing I wouldn't win that fight.

"A vampire. Did Laurent tell you about the new attack last night?" Patrick took the change of subject without skipping a beat.

"He mentioned it in a text this morning. That's all."

Patrick's lips twitched slightly. "Well, clearly he didn't trust you enough to give you the full report, then."

"I can't go tonight anyway," I replied, ignoring his not-so-subtle insult. "I need to do my own investigation for the mission."

"Oh, yeah?" Patrick's sly grin dropped. "We won't be able to cover you tonight."

"I don't need any backup. I've got this."

"So you say. And yet, you were cornered by two werewolves just this week. You think you can take on the Lycan King on your own?" He stalked closer, trying to use his height to intimidate me. It didn't work. It hadn't since I was a kid.

Raising my chin, I met his gaze. "I did last night, didn't I?"

Patrick visibly recoiled as if my sleeping with a supernatural was one of the worst things I could do. In his mind, it probably was. He was too much like our father. He would never stoop so low. Never put himself in that position. If he was alone with a supernatural being, it would end up with his blade in their heart.

"Don't call me if you get into any trouble," Patrick replied coldly. "I won't take the blame for your failure."

"You won't," I replied, standing my ground, my eyes never leaving his.

He studied me for a moment, an emotion I couldn't identify darkening his gaze. "You're running out of time, Sydney. We need proof that Noah Solvmane is leading this rebellion."

"Wait. What?" I replied, trying to process his words. "Father never said EH believed Noah was leading a damn rebellion. When did you all come to this conclusion?"

"You really are pathetic, aren't you?" The statement seemed to be his last as he moved towards me, my body instinctively moving away from the door to get out of his way. I wasn't pathetic, but my brother most certainly was an asshole.

"Just fucking answer the question, Patrick," I finally snapped, watching as he stopped in his tracks. His shoulders rising and falling with his heavy breaths before he finally looked over his shoulder at me with a bored expression as if he'd expected me to not know what was going on.

"We've always had our suspicions that the Lycan King was doing something he shouldn't. We just never knew who he was. Until now."

"I haven't found anything that linked Noah to these attacks. We don't even know if it is an actual rebellion," I argued.

"Oh yes, we do," Patrick snarled, turning on me. Out of habit, I took a step back. "The amount of attacks across the United States have gone up in the last two months alone. That's too many to be a coincidence. Sure, we've had our rogues now and then, but this is different. If you'd been paying attention, you'd know this."

"I've only been in the field for, what, a few weeks?" I countered. "Maybe if I was given a little more information, I would know."

"You're given what you need to know, and that's all," Patrick replied, voice going deadly quiet. "Get what you can tonight and report to father tomorrow. You're already testing his patience."

I fought the urge to stick my tongue out at his back. Or wedge my blade between his shoulders. However, I didn't. Instead, I stood there quietly watching as my brother slammed the door to my apartment, making me wince as the walls rattled. I wouldn't let him get to me. I couldn't. I'd suspected that EH believed Noah might have had something to do with the rising attacks, but now my brother had just confirmed it. He'd walked right into my little mental trap. It was the only way I ever got information out of him.

I needed to somehow find the link between Noah and this potential rebellion. Clearly, work wasn't going to reveal anything. Everything there was too clean. Too tidy. Which meant I would need to go to the one place he would feel he wouldn't need to be protected.

I needed to find a way into his house without being caught.

The vibration in my hand startled me out of my thoughts. I knew it wouldn't be Patrick, or my father, considering he'd checked in that morning already. Glancing at the screen, I held my breath.

Noah.

Oh God. He was going to fire me. Wait... it was Saturday? What did he want?

I dreaded opening his message, my thumb hovering over it before I finally gathered up enough courage.

Meet at my house today at 12 to go over the Anderson deal.

His address was listed below that. Short and to the point. No emotion whatsoever. And yet, butterflies fluttered in my stomach, making their way through my chest. I couldn't tell if he regretted what he did last night, but at least I wasn't being fired.

And now I had my way in.

SOLVMANE MANOR

SYDNEY

I don't know what I was expecting when I arrived at Noah's house, but it wasn't this. I stood outside an iron gate, a wrap-around drive wound up to the front door of a two-story mini-mansion. I mean, I knew Noah was loaded, and I was no stranger to money myself, but it just felt... odd. Like it didn't really fit him.

The house itself looked bright and airy. A porch wrapped around the lower half, porch swing included. Large windows covered the white siding, sheer curtains hanging over the glass. Shrubs and bushes lined the porch, the scent of flowers heavy in the air. I could smell them even at the gate.

How the hell was I supposed to get in there?

I glanced around the iron bars. There was no button, no call pad. Nothing that would allow me to announce my arrival, causing me to stand there awkwardly, trying to figure out how I would go about this when the gates finally creaked open. They slowly rolled to the side, disappearing into the fence posts lining the entire property, which was huge.

Stepping through the gates, my shoes crunched over the gravel as I made my way up the driveway. I didn't have a car or anything considering I lived in the city, so an Uber was the only way to get to his place—which cost a fortune, I might add. It didn't even bring me to the house, which was a problem considering the shoes I was wearing. Wedges had proven to be a bad idea, but I had to go all out if my plan had even an iota of a chance to work. It's not like I could just walk into his house and snoop around. I needed to get him off his guard, and what better way to knock a man off his game than to dress to impress?

The off-white satin baby-doll dress I wore fell just to the middle of my thighs in stiff pleats, the neckline plunging between my breasts, revealing way more than it had a right to. Even the cinched waist just below the v-neck was extravagant,decorated with small diamonds that had been cut into the fabric, hinting at some skin. A little dressy, but still casual enough to get away with it.

By the time I made it to the house, I was cursing at my shoe choice for the day. My footsteps, heavy on the wooden steps, my stomach fluttering in tune with the beat. Before my knuckles could even knock against the door, the screen swung open. Noah towered over me, one arm against the door frame. His biceps flexed as he leaned over, eyes raking down my body.

"You're late."

Of course I was.

He seemed to force himself to turn away, his eyes lingering on me for just a second too long. Holding my breath, I followed him into his house, curious what he had planned for me. Noah didn't even wait for me to get oriented. He headed straight up the stairs, leading the way to the second floor. I scurried after him just to catch up, my brain trying to commit every inch of the home to memory as if this would be the only time I'd ever get to see it.

There were no pictures on the white walls besides a few minimalist paintings. In fact, it seemed his whole house was just... completely different from him. Where his office was dark and brooding with absolutely no life to it... this house was white and airy. The open layout and floral decor screamed a woman's touch. Something that made me wonder if someone else had decorated this house, maybe the woman in the photo from his office.

"Where are we going?" I asked nervously, eyeing the second-floor landing.

Noah glanced over his shoulder, gray eyes flashing. "To the library. Is that a problem?"

"You have a library?" I didn't mean for it to come out sounding so incredulous. But I really didn't peg him as a reader.

"It also serves as an office at times," Noah replied. He turned right, heading toward the first door in the hall. It didn't go unnoticed by me how clipped the conversation was with him. I had slept with him last night out of a moment of weakness, but perhaps I was reading too much into things. I enjoyed it... more than I should have. But it was just a one-night stand.

So why did his silence bother me so much?

I didn't get a good look at the room until I was in it. Much cozier than the rest of the house, the large room had a beige velvet sofa with matching chairs huddled around a rectangular coffee table. Bookshelves had been built into the walls, lining three of them while leaving the fourth open to house a fireplace. It wasn't lit now, but I could just picture how much homier it made the room when it was. Another door sat just beside the fireplace, though it was closed.

"What's behind that door?" I asked.

"My office," Noah replied curtly. He didn't even bother looking to see what I was talking about.

Instead, he took a seat in one of the chairs, pulling a folio from the table and into his lap. "Shall we get started?" He eyed me as I carefully sat at the edge of the couch, trying to cover my knees with my dress skirt. Unsuccessfully, I might add.

Lightning fissured down my spine as I caught his gaze locked onto my knees, trailing over the pleats of the skirt that hung over my thighs.

Clearly, he liked what he saw.

Bingo.

Now I just needed him to actually drop his guard. Maybe even leave the room for a bit so I could snoop around. He'd gotten the upper hand the last time we were alone together, but I wasn't going to let that happen again. And now I knew where his personal office was—the exact place I needed to look around.

He. Just. Needed. To. Leave.

"Are you ready to begin?" Noah asked again, slower this time, as if I had been too slow to understand him the first time.

"Yeah, I am." Heat flared across my cheeks. Covering my slip-up, I held out my hand, waiting for him to hand me the files. "I'm assuming I'll need to look those over?" I continued, raising an eyebrow when he didn't move.

"Yes, you will," he replied, clearing his throat as he passed the portfolio over. "We'll need a clear plan on integrating Anderson's business into our own."

"I thought you already had that all figured out," I muttered.

"If you'll read the files, you'll see that I do," Noah replied smugly. Glancing up, I caught the corners of his lips turning up into a smirk of amusement before I let my eyes drift back to the portfolio once more.

"So what do I need to do, then?"

"I just wanted you to make sure my plan made sense." He stated.

Scanning the first page, the legal jargon and confusing lingo made my brain spin. It wasn't like I was stupid. There were just a hell of a lot of words on that page that probably didn't need to be there. Half of it I could understand. It wasn't too complicated. Noah wanted to utilize Anderson's transportation business to aid local businesses in the poorer areas of New York City—both supernatural-owned and human-owned. There were a few names on there that I recognized from EH's database.

"Overall, it looks pretty simple," I said slowly, flicking to the next page.

Noah drew a breath, as if he were about to say more when his phone went off. "Excuse me." He rose from the chair swiftly, his phone screen lighting up as he put it to his ear. "Hello?"

I waited until he'd closed the library door after him to bolt from the couch. Sneaking over to the office door, I jiggled the handle, unsurprised to find it locked. Without missing a beat, I slid the bobby pin from my hair, releasing it from its duty to hold back the fiery waves. There was a soft click and my small set of lock picks flicked out.

Handy.

Very handy.

It didn't take me too long to jiggle the handle open and slip inside. I left it open just a crack. Just in case. Turning around, I paused. This room wasn't as bare as the rest of the house. More shelves lined the walls on either side of the desk. A flat, low-lying shelf made of dark wood hung just behind the office chair. A thick, blood-red rug had been laid out over the wooden floors, twin chairs of black velvet sitting just on the other side of the desk.

I moved around the edge of the desk, careful not to touch anything. At first, my eyes scanned the desktop, trying to see if there was anything worthy enough of my time to rifle through. But then I caught sight of the photos along the shelf.

There were three in all; two with a single woman, and one with her and Noah. I slowed, stopping just before the photos. My hand reached out, pausing just inches away from the glassy surfaces of the frames. Noah looked so happy in the center image, his teeth flashing brilliantly as he held the woman in his arms. I recognized her right away—the same woman from his office photo.

It took me a few minutes to piece it all together.

If Noah was indeed a Lycan...then this must be his mate. Except I'd never seen her around the office, and I certainly didn't think anyone else was in the house right now. At least, not as far as I could tell. Which means...

"Find what you're looking for?"

I whipped around at the sound of Noah's voice, knowing I'd screwed up. There was no malice in his words, but I could feel the silent anger and disappointment rolling off him in waves as he stood in the entrance to the office, leaning against the door frame with predatory eyes.

"I-I-the door was unlocked," I muttered. "I wanted to get a pen in case I needed to make notes."

"The door was unlocked," he replied flatly, clearly not believing me.

Another excuse was on the tip of my tongue before something else slipped out. "Who's the woman in the picture?"

"None of your business," Noah growled.

"Is that your—wife?" I nearly tripped over the word, almost slipping up.

Noah hesitated a beat. "Yes."

My heart had dropped into my stomach at his words, but making sure to keep my emotions in check, I sighed before nodding my head. "Is she here? I'd love to meet her. I promise I won't cause trouble—"

"No, she isn't," he snapped, his tone getting a darker the more I seemed to talk about her, which completely confused me.

"I promise I don't want to cause problems—"

His lip curled, a look of pure hatred flicking over his face. That caused me to shiver as the temperature in the room seemed to drop at leas ten degrees. "You don't need to worry about her, Sydney. She was taken from me."

I knew what that meant without even having to ask. Taken from him. Probably hunted down. There would have been no other explanation. Not many humans knew supernaturals existed. But Elite Humanity did. And they'd been on Noah's tail for years trying to find out who he truly was. My stomach sank.

"I'm sorry." My words came out as nothing more than a whisper. But I knew he heard me anyway.

With a sharp shake of his head, Noah shrugged off my apology. "It was a long time ago," he replied coldly. "Now, if you don't mind, I'd like to get back to work."

Ducking my head, I slipped past him, scurrying out of the room. His eyes bounced between me and the door handle, and I knew he didn't fully believe my story of the door just being unlocked. I'm sure he was the type of person to meticulously check and see if the doors are actually locked when he leaves.

But if he suspected anything, he didn't show it.

"Of course," I replied, keeping an eye on him as I made my way back to the place I had once been sitting. My mind raced a mile a minute as I hoped he would let the situation go and decide it wasn't worth considering any longer. Though the way he stared at me as he made his way to the chair across from me made me nervous.

There was a cold gleam in his eyes that screamed suspicion. A look that made the hair on the back of my neck stand on edge as I tried to focus on the paperwork in my hand. I was getting way to close to him and I wasn't actually afraid, I couldn't let go of the nagging feeling of impending doom that floated in the back of my mind.

Get your shit together! I mentally told myself. *You can do this.*

Taking a deep breath, I placed the edge of the pen to my lips, biting at it gently as I let my gaze slid up to meet his. "So... how would you like to do this?"

Mentally facepalming myself, I watched the corner of his lips twitch as a smirk lined his face. Something about that gaze made my thighs press together, and when he opened his mouth, I was thrown once again into flashbacks of how he had ravished me before.

"However you want to, Princess."

Because that totally didn't just sound provocative.

BLOOD & WORRY

Noah

I kept telling myself that women were naturally curious. That Sydney's blatant disregard for locked, closed doors had nothing to do with the rat investigating in my company at the moment. It wasn't as if I'd caught her snooping through my drawers or my computer. She'd simply been standing there, staring at the pictures on the shelf behind the desk as if surprised to find any remnants of my life.

That's what I kept telling myself, anyway.

Yet, as we sat there going over the documents I'd prepared months ago for Anderson's company, I couldn't completely ignore the darker thoughts that slowly crept from the back of my mind. The suspicion my brother had planted there from the start hadn't gone away entirely, despite me finding no evidence that Sydney had anything to do with Elite Humanity or even knowing that supernaturals existed. Sure, there was something off about her, something both my beast and I couldn't ignore, but that didn't mean she was the culprit.

A knock sounded at the library door, interrupting my thoughts. Across from me, Sydney jumped slightly, her fingers curling over the papers in her lap.

"Come in," I called, my eyes never leaving her as I tracked each nervous movement, the rise and fall of her breath, the sound of her heart skipping a beat. All of it resonated in my ears.

Just as the images of her from last night resonated through my head.

My butler, James, stepped into the room. It sounded far fancier than it was. James had been working for my family for years, caring for the house while we were away, and making sure I actually ate each night. He looked older than me, though I'd been around for far longer. His balding head still clung to a few wispy, gray hairs and his skin was lined with wrinkles. He moved slower than molasses in January, but he was dependable and loyal.

Adjusting the collar of his button-up, James cleared his throat. "Lunch is ready on the back porch, sir. As requested."

Sydney's head snapped back around to me, a look of confusion flashing across her face. "Lunch?"

"I figured we would get hungry eventually." Setting the papers aside, I rose from the chair. "We can finish this after."

She was hesitant for a moment, before she followed suit, smoothing her skirt as she stood. It didn't matter how much I was around her, or how irritated the entire situation surrounding her made me, every time she moved I was captivated by her beauty. Following me out of the library in silence, an air of nervousness still clinging to her, she made her way with me towards the back porch where lunch awaited us. Whether it was because she'd been caught snooping or the idea of having lunch with me set her off, I couldn't tell. Nothing about this was normal. She'd started off as my human secretary, nothing more than someone to fill the shoes that had been previously abandoned each month, but now...

I'd slept with her. And I couldn't take that back even if I wanted to.

Which I didn't.

Leading Sydney down the stairs and through the kitchen to the back porch, I contemplated our current situation while she seemed to admire the scenery. It had been renovated a few years ago, though I was never out here much. Along, glass table was set up to the left of the fire pit that was never used. Black metal chairs sat around the table, freshly dusted. Atop the table, a lunch spread had been laid out perfectly. A roasted chicken sat in the center of the table, cut into orderly slices. A salad bowl had been placed beside that, a few dressing choices arranged around it. There was a pot of tomato soup, and a basket of bread rolls that still steamed as if they'd just come from the oven. Overall, James had done a fairly decent job in making a normal lunch look... well, normal.

Pulling out a chair, I waited for Sydney to take a seat before taking my place at the head of the table. James moved in, serving her a plate efficiently before setting it in front of her before she even had a chance to argue. When that was done, I waved him away.

"This seems to be a lot for just the two of us," Sydney noted, eyeing her plate of food.

"I wasn't sure what you'd like," I replied, placing food on my own plate. I wasn't hungry—I'd eat later when she was gone—but I didn't want her to feel awkward.

"Well... thank you." She picked up a fork, gently stabbing at the chicken on her plate. I watched her silently, waiting for her to take the first bite.

When she caught me staring, she paused, fork freezing halfway to her lips. Sighing, she set it back down. "Are we ever going to talk about—"

"There's nothing to talk about." I knew what she wanted to discuss. I just wasn't ready to have that conversation. What was I going to say? That I'd slept with her to look through her apartment just to make sure she wasn't a spy? That sleeping with her had felt much more than that, surprising me? That there was nothing I wanted more than to sweep this food off the damn table and take her again right there?

I couldn't say any of that.

Sydney's lips parted as if to argue, but she didn't have a chance.

"Sir?" James reappeared at the back door, his face lined with tension. The smell of blood hit my nose through the open door, heavy and familiar.

Before I knew it, I was already on my feet. "What is it?"

Sydney glanced between us warily. "Is everything alright?"

I ignored her, following James back into the house. My brother was in the living room, leaning heavily against the wall. His arm was wrapped around his side. The smell of blood was overpowering here and no wonder—he was covered in it. Red stained his clothes around his torso, his arms, and face. Pain was etched onto his face, visibly clear.

"What the hell happened?" I growled, stalking forward. I grabbed his free arm, throwing it over my shoulder before heading for the stairs. Sydney couldn't see this.

"What's going on?" Her voice was calm, eyes darting between my brother and I.

My eyes shut briefly. Too late.

Glancing at Sydney over my shoulder, I found her standing in the entrance to the living room, horrified. "Nothing. Go back outside," I snapped, before turning to James. "Get her out of here."

James tried to herd her back through the kitchen, but she avoided him. "Noah, what's going on?" she repeated. "Is he alright?" Clearly, he wasn't.

She tried to side-step James, her eyes zeroing in on Lawson. There was no surprise in her eyes. No, look of fear. There was nothing but cold calculation. As if this was nothing she hadn't seen before.

"Sydney, get the hell out." I didn't mean for it to come out so harshly, but I was a little preoccupied with my brother, whose strength was quickly failing. I could feel his life bleeding out on me, his legs shaking as they tried to hold them up.

Without looking back, I flung him over my shoulder and darted up the stairs. The guest room he usually stayed in was still made up for him, just in case. The sheets had been freshly washed and made, looking immaculate, though they wouldn't be for long. I rolled him onto his back, ripping his blood-stained shirt open. Swearing, I studied the wound.

Several bullet holes were scattered across his abdomen and, from the way the surrounding skin had turned black, I knew they were made of silver. Leaving him on the bed, I raced back to my room for my medical supplies. But James had already beaten me there. He tossed the kit to me, grabbing gauze and bandages from beneath my bathroom counter.

"Where's Sydney?" He shouldn't be here. He should be downstairs making sure Sydney wouldn't stick her damn nose into this mess. The last thing I needed was for my secretary to suspect that I was anything more than a CEO of a logistics company.

"She left." James shrugged, grabbing one last roll of bandages before closing the door. He stood, bones creaking, as he herded me out into the bedroom. "Gone."

"She left?" I asked incredulously. "Just like that?" It didn't make any sense.

"Said clearly it was time for her to go," James replied, pushing me out the door and into the hall.

I'd have to deal with that later. Right now, my brother needed me. We hurried back into the guest room, getting to work. James deftly cleaned the wounds before grabbing a pair of tweezers. His hands were steady as he quickly pulled each bullet from Lawson's body. To his credit, Lawson kept it together, though I'm sure his lack of reaction was more to him nearly passing out than his ability to withstand the pain.

Lawson was a trooper, but even I wouldn't be able to manage if I had been clear minded. Silver was deathly to us. Not as potent to us as a typical Werewolf, but if left too long it would kill us in the end just the same.

James deposited the silver bullets on the bedside table before I quickly covered the wounds with gauze. It would take some time before the silver was fully out of his system, but he shouldn't have any trouble healing after. James helping me to move Lawson's body as I wrapped the bandages around his center, making sure they weren't too tight.

"Noah..." Lawson said weakly, but thankfully still conscious.

"What happened?" I asked again, a slight edge to my voice.

"There was an ambush." He closed his eyes, another emotion flashing across his face. Regret. Loss.

"How many did we lose?"

"All of them."

I swore again, my fist connecting with the wall before I could stop myself. I'd told him not to do anything stupid. Clearly, he hadn't listened to me. He'd probably taken out the usual amount for a security sweep, which means we lost around eight men tonight.

Eight.

I didn't ask who they were. Not yet. I needed time to process this. Clearly, they'd run into Elite Humanity, though they shouldn't have been attacked. Not like this. If I could even call it that. Because this wasn't an attack—this was a massacre.

"Is she... still here?" Lawson asked quietly.

"Who?"

"That girl. The secretary."

For a moment, I'd forgotten about Sydney. "No," I replied flatly. "She left."

"And you don't think that's odd?" Lawson replied, eyeing me. "That she would just leave after seeing me like this? That she didn't freak out?"

I didn't have a good answer to that. He was right, in a way. Any normal human would freak out and most likely call the cops, or at least an ambulance. Sydney had done neither. In fact, she hadn't even seemed that surprised when she saw my brother bleeding out in the living room. She'd seemed... calm.

"I'll worry about that later," I said finally.

Lawson glanced up at me, lips thinning. "You might need to worry about that sooner rather than later."

"What do you mean?" I asked confused, my eyes watching as my brother cringed again from the pain. Before he could answer, his eyes closed and he was lost to the sleep he so desperately needed. There had been a warning to his tone I hadn't missed, and perhaps he was right.

I needed to start worrying now, because if I wasn't careful—she would be my downfall.

UNDERSTANDING MY PURPOSE

SYDNEY

I knew what had happened the minute I saw Noah's brother in the living room. At least, I assumed it was his brother. They certainly shared the same rugged, mysterious look; black hair and light eyes that drew you in and made you forget to breathe.

Noah had tried to keep me from seeing it, probably worried that I'd call the cops or an ambulance. But I did none of that. As soon as they were gone, I excused myself, dipping under the butler's arms and racing for the front door. I knew I should have stayed to figure out what had happened, but I didn't care. I needed to get out of there.

Besides, as I'd said, I already knew what happened.

I could smell the scent of silver beneath the smell of blood. I'd grown up around the stuff for far too long not to recognize it. And the only people who would be shooting silver bullets at known supernaturals was Elite Humanity. I would have bet everything I knew exactly who had done this as well.

"I wanted to see if you'd like to go hunting with us tonight, or if you were too busy with your new distraction."

My brother had gone hunting last night, probably bringing my sister along. They had to be the ones who had done this—I didn't know anyone else who would be stupid enough to shoot a Lycan that hadn't broken the rules. Because that's not what we did. We only made sure supernaturals followed the laws we had set in place to protect humans. We weren't supposed to break them ourselves.

I called my uber driver as I raced down the long drive. He wouldn't take long. I'd told him to park down the road and wait until I called when he'd dropped me off. Now, I stood in front of the gates, trying to figure out how to open them. Clearly, Noah or his butler wasn't about to open them for me. Biting back a sigh of frustration, I slipped off my wedges and tossed them through the bars.

Looks like I was climbing.

It didn't take me long. Thankfully, I was still able to scramble over the bars, even in a dress, though I'm sure it looked anything but graceful. By the time my feet hit the paved road, my driver had finally managed to get there. Without looking back, I jumped into the car, barking orders to head back to my apartment.

The entire ride home, my mind replayed the scene in the living room over and over again. His brother had been injured. Badly. I saw the amount of blood and the paleness of his skin as he leaned against the wall. I saw the look of carefully controlled fear on Noah's face. It all hit me like a sack of bricks. This was real. This was what it looked like from the other side. Noah might have been a monster, but he still had a family. He still had a life.

And my family had almost taken that away from him… again.

I didn't know what had happened to his mate, but I could make a pretty good guess. Noah had said she'd been taken from him.

Whatever had happened, it hadn't been expected based on his reaction to me being there. It was still a sore subject, something he wasn't ready to face just yet.

A strange feeling twisted in my stomach—one I'd never felt before. It crept from the depths of my consciousness, strangling my lungs until it felt as if I were drowning in the back seat of the town car.

Guilt.

I felt guilty that I had something to do with Noah's loss and his brother's pain. My own family had done this, which felt wrong. All wrong. We were supposed to help people. To keep humans safe. But we also weren't supposed to just go out and hunt down supernaturals who weren't doing anything wrong. And I had a feeling that Noah's brother wasn't breaking the law when he'd been attacked.

This was all wrong.

The driver pulled up in front of my apartment building, letting me out. Shutting the door behind me, I hurried up the steps to get to the elevator. I needed time to process all of this, to figure out what my next steps were. I still had my mission to complete—to prove that Noah was behind the attacks, but it felt... off. Because what if it wasn't Noah behind the attacks? What if it was one of us?

I dismissed the idea as soon as it popped into my head. Or, at least I tried to. It wouldn't make sense for an EH operative to coerce supernaturals to attack humans. It went against everything we stood for. But images of Noah's brother kept flashing through my mind. It was also against our laws to attack supernaturals who were not breaking our rules and yet that had clearly happened.

None of this was making any sense.

I froze as I stepped off the elevator. Melissa leaned against the wall beside my front door, studying her nails. Her perfectly straight blond hair was swept over her shoulder, blue eyes narrowed as they locked onto me. There were still flecks of blood along her fingers, brilliant against her pale skin.

"Took you long enough." She glanced at my front door with a sour look on her face. "Updated system I'm guessing?"

"What did you do?" I had no patience for her games today.

Her eyes scanned my outfit, lip curling. "Did you have a nice time on your little date?"

"It wasn't a date," I replied, cringing. I hadn't meant to feed into it, but it had slipped out before I could stop it. "What did you do?" I repeated.

"Nothing," Melissa replied, shrugging one petite shoulder. "We just went hunting, is all. Patrick said you'd turned him down."

"I had other things to do."

"Like sleeping with the enemy?"

Her words stopped me cold. I stood my ground, though, meeting her gaze with a cold look of my own. "That's none of your business. How I handle my own mission is none of your concern."

"Just think of how disappointed father will be when I tell him." She sighed dramatically, pushing off the wall. "Maybe then he'll stop this nonsense and pull you off entirely." So that was her plan. I always knew she wanted me out of the picture, but to use this against me?

"You're not going to blackmail me," I hissed, anger rising. "Tell father anything you want. It won't matter."

"Won't it?" Melissa cocked her head, studying me. "You don't think he'll deem this unprofessional and pull you from the mission entirely? He told you to get information from the suspect—not sleep with him."

"I'm sure you've done worse."

I felt it before I even registered her movement. My cheek stung, tears pricking my eyes. Melissa towered over me, cheeks reddening as anger flashed through her eyes.

"Say that again," she growled, "I dare you."

I stood my ground, meeting her gaze. "I'm sure you've done what you had to do, Melissa. I certainly wouldn't be surprised to hear the things you've done during missions."

"You have no idea what you're talking about," she hissed. "I would never lower myself just to get the job done." Realizing I'd gotten the better of her, she straightened, flicking her hair back over her shoulder. "Besides, I'm competent enough to achieve my goals without stooping so low. Clearly, you were not. If you continue this, you'll be no better than our mother."

"What?" Her words knocked the air from my lungs. "What are you talking about?"

"Oh, that's right. You don't know." A cruel smile tugged at the corners of her lips as she feigned sympathy. "I guess you were too young to remember."

I didn't want to give in, didn't want to give her any reason to have something to hold over me. But she knew she had me. "Explain."

Her shoulder brushed mine as she headed toward the elevator. "I'll let you in on a little family secret, dear sister." Her perfectly manicured nail tapped the down button. Glancing over her shoulder, she flashed a smile. "Mother wasn't killed in action. In fact, she'd never killed a supernatural in her life. But she did love one."

The floor dipped beneath my feet, the hallway walls closing in. "What are you talking about?" The words sounded strange to my ears. Warbled as if underwater.

"She fell in love with a Werewolf," Melissa said slowly, enunciating each word. "She abandoned us for a monster. Her little stunt nearly ruined Elite Humanity. Nearly killed you, even."

"You're lying." She had to be. Father hadn't said anything about this to me. All I'd been told was that she'd been killed in the line of duty, protecting us from a Werewolf who had threatened our family. She'd died a hero, doing what she had to to keep us safe.

"Am I?" Melissa asked innocently. The elevator doors opened. Stepping inside, she turned, hitting the button for the lobby. "Maybe the apple really doesn't fall far from the tree."

I could only watch as the doors closed, the image of my sister laughing burned into my mind. I didn't want to believe her. Didn't want to play into her games. But something told me she wasn't lying. She had no reason to. Not about this.

Feeling sick to my stomach, I stumbled toward my front door, fumbling with my keys. It took me a few minutes to unlock the door. Stepping inside, I quickly closed and locked it behind me, pressing my back against the solid wood until the room stopped spinning.

I didn't have much time to pull myself together. My phone vibrated in my bag, alerting me to a call. Wary, I pulled it out, reading the name on the screen.

Crap.

"Hello?"

"We need to talk." My father's voice felt as cold as it sounded. Chills swept down my spine. "Be outside and ready in twenty minutes."

"Ready for what?" I asked, forcing the words from my throat.

"We're going hunting."

He hung up before I had a chance to reply. A heaviness settled in the pit of my stomach. My father never went out hunting anymore. He rarely left the EH headquarters. For him to come all the way out here, just for me, was not a good sign. Maybe Melissa had already told him what I'd done and she hadn't been trying to blackmail me. I wouldn't have put it past her to do so.

But it's not like I could tell him no.

Pushing away from the door, I dropped my purse on the couch as I headed toward the bedroom. Guess I was going hunting.

HUNTING WITH DAD

SYDNEY

New York City settled into its nightly chaos around me as I trudged down the street to the meeting point. I had to be dropped off on the other side of the city, far away from the safety of lights and people. Here, the sounds of cars honking, the sirens, the people—it was all muted as if in a dream.

Or a nightmare.

Shadows crept along the sidewalk, skulking between the warehouse along the river. Moonlight glistened over the water, swallowed by the darkness beneath the calm waves. It smelled like salt this far to the west, the light breeze carrying the sea over land. It would have been peaceful had I not been about to meet up with the devil himself.

My steps slowed as I neared the location he'd sent me, glancing around nervously. This had to be the right place. It seemed like his usual MO; a secluded area with more darkness than light, far enough away from humans to avoid detection. While my father had made it his life's mission to protect people, he didn't particularly like them. Or being around them. Especially when hunting.

I wasn't sure what we'd be doing tonight, though I could guess. I'd heard the rumors, seen the news headings. There'd been more and more attacks this week, people disappearing left and right. The humans thought it was just a rise in crime or human trafficking. I knew those people were never going to come back. Or, if they did, they wouldn't be the same.

Checking the time on my watch, I paced up and down the sidewalk. He was late. And he was never late.

"Daughter."

Whipping around, I came face-to-face with Laurent. He towered over me, graying hair buzzed close to his scalp. His blue eyes were piercing, even in the darkness. It was evident that my siblings were his children. Patrick had the same strong jaw and sharp nose. Melissa, the same ice-filled blue eyes. If I didn't know any better, I would have guessed that I'd been adopted at some point.

He was dressed in all black, the EH logo stitched onto the left breast of his leather jacket. I could see a bulge on his left side, his dark shirt hiding the gun from sight. I was sure he had more weapons on him somewhere. He never left the house without at least five. Just in case.

I'd dressed similarly, knowing we would need to blend in. I'd pulled my wild hair back into a ponytail before braiding it. My black boots were light despite how sturdy they were. My blade was strapped to my side, just beneath my own jacket. That was the only weapon I'd brought, but it didn't matter. That was the only one I needed.

"Why did you want me to come out tonight?" I asked warily. "I've been giving you updates."

He snorted, his eyes never leaving mine. "I wouldn't call those updates."

When he refused to say more, I sighed. "What are we hunting tonight?"

"There's been reports of a vampire hunting out here. Taking its victims to one of these warehouses to dispose of them." He scanned the row of buildings as if they might reveal the answer.

He always referred to the supernaturals as "it". To him, they weren't people. Only monsters. My sister's words came back to me as I followed him down the sidewalk. If what she said was true, then it wasn't surprising he thought that way. That any of them thought that way. My siblings, my father—they probably all believed our mother abandoned us for a creature that should never have been alive in the first place.

"How long have you been tracking this vamp?" I asked, trying not to think about whether or not my sister was telling the truth. There was no way in hell I'd ask my father and risk his wrath.

"A few days. The call was put out on Monday."

"And will it just be us two?" I hedged, feeling more anxious by the minute. We weren't ever supposed to go hunting with only two people. There had to at least be a team of four just in case something went sideways.

"Just us two." Laurent barely glanced at me. "Unless that's a problem?"

I straightened up. "No, not a problem at all." I had to prove to him that I could do this, even if this all went against our protocols. Besides, I was with the man who enforced them anyway. It's not like I would get in trouble for breaking the rules.

"In here." He jiggled the handle of one of the doors.

The warehouse it belonged to looked empty. A few windows had been knocked out, the metal siding rusting slightly from years of abandonment. The rusted lock on the door broke easily in my father's hands. Shoving his shoulder against the door, it took him a few minutes to budge it open.

Which gave me more time to worry. Something wasn't right about all this.

Stepping inside, the temperature seemed to drop. It was colder here and less humid. The main floor of the warehouse was empty with a thick layer of dust that settled on top of crates and other objects I couldn't make out. It didn't look like anything had been disturbed in here for a while. Beside us, metal stairs led to a second floor that overlooked the main room. Catwalks lined the walls, leading back into the darkness. I couldn't tell just how big this warehouse was, but it felt huge.

"You take the second floor," my father muttered.

I knew the drill. I tried to ascend the stairs as quietly as possible. I still wasn't sure why my father had brought me tonight, or what he hoped to gain from this, but I wasn't about to forget my training. If he was here to berate me, he wasn't about to find fault in my duties.

Stepping out onto the catwalk, I crouched as I went, keeping an eye both on the path in front of me and my father below. He stalked forward, gun raised in front of him as he went, sticking to the shadows. Rays of moonlight streamed in through the window, dust particles swirling in the empty space. Crates covered in tarp had been left behind near the back, hiding a few doors that led to only God knew where.

If a vampire had brought its victims here, I couldn't tell. It was too quiet. Too empty. Though it would have been a good place if I was a supernatural killer.

A crash pulled me from my thoughts, making me jump. It had come from the first floor, in the back. My father took off, wasting no time. I hurried to keep up with him, boots pounding on the catwalk. There was no use in trying to be subtle now. The vampire probably knew we were here.

I caught sight of a shadow lunging toward Laurent. Before I could shout a warning, he was already ducking, his gun going off in a staccato. Light flashed, making my vision blurry before it all fell dark again. Glancing down, Laurent was nowhere to be seen. Neither was the shadow.

"Screw this." Ignoring protocols, I vaulted over the railing, climbing down before I let myself fall. As soon as my boots hit the ground, I took off around the empty crates. A door banged shut to my right, followed by more shots. Leave it to my father to face off against a vampire on his own. Just before I reached the door, I stumbled, my boot hitting something heavy.

Not something.

Someone.

The woman was long dead, her eyes blank and glassy. Her skin was paler than the moonlight, smeared with blood around her throat. Golden locks fell in soft waves around her shoulders, her lips tinged blue. She'd been gone for a while from the looks of it. Like the vamp had its meal before dragging her here.

Swearing, I could barely hear the noises of a fight over the sound of my racing heart. Sweat pricked at my palms as I raced forward, heaving the door open. It led into a long hallway. I caught sight of my father disappearing around the bend just as another shot echoed down the corridor.

Adrenaline raced through my veins as I ran after him. He shouldn't have gone off on his own, even if he was the freaking leader of EH. Even just one vamp alone was dangerous. I pushed myself to go faster, finally making it around the corner.

My father had the vampire cornered. There were no doors at this end of the hallway. No windows. No way out. The vampire turned to face him, fangs bared.

"Elite Humanity scum," he hissed, red eyes flashing. There was blood smeared along his lips and fingers. His hair was so blond it looked almost silver, even in the dark. "You going to take me in now?"

I tensed. It hadn't occurred to me before, but Laurent didn't have any of the usual handcuffs and chains we would have used to secure a supernatural to take them in. All he had was that damn gun. I'd been too preoccupied to think of it before, too nervous about the reason he'd ask me to go hunting in the first place.

My father cocked his head slightly, eyes narrowing. "No."

He moved too fast for me to register what was going on. The gun went off once. Twice. Three times. The silver immobilized the vamp, pinning him where he stood hissing in pain. Laurent lunged forward, withdrawing a stake from the inside of his jacket.

"Wait—no!" I froze, watching as the wood sank into the vampire's chest. His screech of anger, of pain, echoed around me, chilling me to the bone.

The vampire's scream choked off, his skin starting to peel and crack. The memory of the vampire I had killed years ago flashing in my mind as I watched the ashes of this creature slowly drop to the floor. Laurent bent to the pile, yanking the stake from the ashes as if this was something he had done a million times. Which confused me because it wasn't what we were taught to do.

"Da—" I tried to shake the fog from my mind. "We're not supposed to do that. We were supposed to take him in. He broke the law, we have to follow it."

"Don't be so naive, Sydney," my father growled, wiping the last of the ash from the stake before he reholstered his gun, turning to face me. "This is what we do. They kill. We kill them."

"But that's—"

"They've become more aggressive. More and more are ignoring our laws. Our rules. Our old way of handling these beasts isn't working anymore." He studied me carefully, those blue eyes of his searing into mine. "This is why I took you out tonight. To show you the consequences of failing to protect those we promised to protect."

Taken back by what he was saying, I stood staring into his icy blue eyes with confusion and hurt within my chest. I knew what he was referring to. It didn't take a genius to figure that out. My father knew I'd slept with Noah, and this was his way of subtly trying to remind me the Lycan King was a monster. That if I wasn't careful people would die as a result of what I was doing with the "monster".

The problem was my father didn't have the slightest clue who Noah was, not that he would ever try to figure it out either. The pain and realization that everything I had been taught growing up was a lie, killed me. Yes, there were bad people out there... but there were also good people too. Not every monster was set out for blood, and even though I was beginning to question what my family was really doing, I was also conflicted.

Did I simply let this go and follow my fathers rules as I should?

Or should I do the right things and tell someone what was going on?

WAKING LAWSON

NOAH

Time and time again, I kept telling myself that I could fix things. That being a leader came with the responsibility of taking care of everyone, that I had to do it on my own. But when my brother came through the door riddled with bullet holes, bleeding out in front of me, I was hit with the realization I was failing him and everyone else who relied on me.

As the Lycan King, it was my job to protect those who couldn't be protected. Yes, I had gone out on the occasional scouting with my brother, but I should have been there with him last night. Instead, I let Sydney cloud my mind and my judgment and let my brother go with eight other men who all died.

Lawson should have died and that thought hit harder than anything.

It took Lawson longer to heal than usual, which didn't surprise me after seeing the amount of silver in his body. I was more surprised that he wasn't out for longer. Sitting beside his bed while he rested, I waited for him to wake up and give a full report of what happened.

I knew who had ambushed them without even asking. There could only be one group that would cause this much damage. One organization that liked to use silver bullets to do their dirty work. Elite Humanity was known for playing dirty. I'd been around long enough to know their whole 'save the humans' was a farce. They were scared humans who lacked power so they'd made their own.

A quality I looked forward to getting rid of one day.

The sun had almost set when Lawson finally came around. He groaned, one eye cracking open just a tad as he realized I was sitting next to him. "You been here long?"

"The whole time," I replied, stretching back into the chair I had placed next to his bed. I hadn't realized how long it had been. My mind had drifted during the time I waited for him to wake up.

"You didn't have to."

"If something happened to you, Shane would murder me."

My younger brother Shane had always been closer to Lawson than I had, which made sense considering after our father died, I had to step up and take his place, leaving Lawson with the need to have someone look after him. That someone turned out to be Shane, who had no problem doing it considering he never wanted to be part of the hierarchy.

Lawson cracked a smile knowing exactly what I was talking about before it turned pained as he slowly sat up in bed. The bandages were still holding on, wrapped around his torso to help with the healing process. His muscles flexed as he moved, rippling beneath his skin as if restless. Which, given his nature, he probably was.

"Does that mean we aren't going to tell him?" he asked, giving me a sideward glance and a smirk as I shook my head.

"And deal with that fall out? No thank you."

Sighing, Lawson's smirk fell as he finally got himself comfortable. "I'm assuming you want to know the whole story?"

"That would be nice." I wasn't going to push him, but I did need to know how serious the situation was. Elite Humanity had never attacked one of my own like this before. Sure, they'd been nabbing supernaturals, but it had always been one-by-one—not a pack.

"We were just out patrolling, trying to see if we could catch wind of any EH pickups that night," Lawson began. He ran a hand through his short hair, blowing out a breath. "We didn't even know they had us surrounded until it was too late. There were way too many of them too. More than usual."

"Were they loaded up?" I asked, leaning forward.

"To the nines," Lawson replied. "Silver fucking everywhere."

A frown tugged "Do you think this was planned?"

"How could it have been? We didn't even know where we'd end up at." Lawson shook his head. "No... it seemed like they'd followed us. Like they were hunting us."

My head snapped up. "What do you mean?"

"They were waiting for us. Patrick and Melissa, along with a few others. They knew we were heading in that direction and cut us off."

"EH is supposed to only step in if a supernatural breaks the laws," I growled.

"Well, clearly they don't follow their own rules," Lawson replied darkly. "Laurent's kids knew what they were doing."

I fell quiet for a moment, trying to process this. If that were true, then we had more problems to deal with than rogue supernaturals.

Elite Humanity was now actively hunting us down and that was never a good thing. They hadn't dared do that for centuries.

"Why do you think it's changed now?" Lawson asked. I hadn't realized I'd spoken that last part out loud. "Do you think they have something to do with these attacks?"

"There's nothing linking them to it. All we know is that they've always been right there to pick up the supernaturals who've attacked humans," I said slowly.

"So they could have done what they did to us tonight. Wait for something to happen. Maybe instigate it."

I didn't like where Lawson was going with this. Elite Humanity claimed to be the protectors of humanity against the monsters that went bump in the night... but that didn't mean they were the good guys. Patrick in particular was a good example. He was too much like his father—ruthless with a toxic mix of calculating and rash.

"What about your secretary? Did you look into her more?" Lawson pressed. "Did she contact you after... seeing me like that?"

"No." My fingers curled into fists. "She did not."

"You sure she didn't go running to the police?"

"They'd be here already."

"Then something's up, brother." Lawson shot me a sharp look. "Any human that doesn't freak out after seeing that has some dark secrets."

"You think she's with Elite Humanity." It wasn't a question.

"She shows up right when we get a tip about a rat in the company? It can't be a coincidence," Lawson continued.

"She had nothing at her house," I told him firmly. "Nothing that indicates she's with Elite Humanity. And I can't just go around accusing people of that. It'll raise too many questions."

"Not to mention, she might think you're insane if you do," Lawson snickered. He did a double-take when I didn't join him. "You like her, don't you?"

I looked away, knowing I wouldn't be able to hide it from him. "I barely know her. She's my secretary and nothing else."

"Holy shit..." I heard the blankets rustle. "You do. I thought after Roya—"

"Don't," I snarled, whipping back around. I got to my feet, smoothing down my shirt. "You need to rest some more. We'll discuss what we're going to do about the attacks and Elite Humanity later."

"Noah—"

I ignored him, closing the bedroom door firmly behind me. As much as I wanted to try and block out his words, they kept coming back. It felt like a betrayal to her—to Roya. Despite how long it's been, I still felt like I couldn't do that to her. Not yet.

But I couldn't ignore whatever this was that I felt toward Sydney either. My beast wouldn't let me. And that was a problem. If she did have a connection to Elite Humanity, if she was the rat in my company, then that would be a very, very serious issue.

One I needed to figure out sooner rather than later.

***

She was late.

I sat in my office, watching the clock on the monitor screen. I knew Sydney wasn't at her desk because I couldn't smell her. My fingers tapped against the desk in time with the seconds that ticked by. She should have been here by now, tapping away at her computer while writing down my daily schedule.

But she wasn't.

My ears pricked at the sound of the elevator door opening. Soft footsteps carried down the hall, but it was the scent of jasmine and roses that alerted me to her presence. She took her sweet time coming down the corridor. Feeling impatient, I stood, pushing my chair back as I stalked toward the door.

I wasn't angry at her for being late. I was more irritated by the situation, by the way I felt about her, and the fact that everything kept pointing to her being the rat in my company.

Something I didn't want to admit.

Throwing open the door, Sydney jumped a little in her seat she had obviously just settled into, her mouth parting slightly. I wasn't sure what I had planned to do when I opened the door, scold her maybe? But the moment she bit gently on her bottom lip, I became fixated on them. Fixated on the idea of tasting her once more, holding her body in my arms.

"You were supposed to clock in five minutes ago," I said icily, shaking off the erotic images flashing through my mind that threatened to derail my composure.

Sydney's eyes flashed with irritation as if she couldn't believe I would come out and say something to her. "I had a late morning."

She looked tired. There were dark circles under her eyes, her wild hair barely tamed in a messy bun. Her fingers tapped against her thigh nervously as she looked away. Something felt… off.

"Did something happen?"

Her head snapped up from where her eyes had drifted off. "No. Nothing. I just didn't sleep well last night. That's all. I'm sorry for being late."

She was lying. I could hear her heartbeat skip a beat, nearly taste the scent of her anxiety in the air. Something had happened, though she clearly wasn't about to tell me. Taking a step closer, I leaned one arm against the wall of the office, towering over her.

Sydney tensed, her eyes cast down as she locked them onto her desk.

"If something happened, you can tell me," I murmured. She was so close now. My beast was practically begging for me to reach out and brush the stray hair from her cheek but I kept my hand solidly by my side, ignoring him.

"Nothing happened," she snapped, voice tight. When she realized who she was talking to, she sighed. "But thank you for asking. I should probably get started on work now…"

Her dismissal was clear enough. I pushed away from the wall, forcing myself to head back into my office. She was hiding something. I could feel it. But I couldn't press her without pushing the boundaries. And if I did that, I might get nothing at all.

I stood there, back pressed against the door, listening to her get to work. Papers rustled across the desk, the keyboard tapped. Her breaths were short, but even. Her heartbeat still not settling.

She was scared.

About what, I had no clue. Unless…

I shook my head, refusing to let Lawson get to me. I still had no proof that she had anything to do with Elite Humanity. And she had seen my brother in a state the other day. Clearly, it had affected her in some way. Perhaps she felt too afraid to go to the police since I was her boss. Or maybe she didn't want to get involved in whatever she thought it was. Either way, something was bothering her.

Settling into my chair, I leaned my elbows against the top of the desk. Sydney wasn't easy to read. Not like other humans. Her usual spark was muted this morning, her light dulled. And I suspected it wasn't just because of what had happened at my house.

No, there was something more going on here.

Picking up my phone, I placed a call to Mr. Grey. He may have been my assistant but he was good at a variety of things. Like reading people, for one. I had known him for over a hundred years and the man had the position he did because of what he was good at, but it had been a very long time since I had asked him to do something like this.

"Yes, sir?" he said as he answered the phone.

"I need you to do me a favor, Grey," I replied, knowing it was now or never if I was going to get to the bottom of things. "I need you to find out what Sydney is hiding."

UNDER COVER IN THE DARK

SYDNEY

The lesson my father tried to teach me clung to my skin like poison. I couldn't shake it. He'd broken the rules. Our rules. Sure, he'd claimed the supernaturals were becoming more aggressive, that more and more of them were shaking off the chains we'd put them in. But something in my gut was telling me that wasn't the truth.

At least not the whole truth.

I was missing something. I just didn't know what it was yet. I'd trusted Elite Humanity my entire life. They *were* my entire life. All I'd ever known was training to become the next EH agent, to help save humanity. But this felt wrong. All wrong.

Noah wasn't the monster I thought he was. At least from what I've seen. None of my searches—either at the company or his house—had led me to anything that would link him to the attacks. In fact, the only evidence I've seen of him doing anything at all was cutting that deal with Anderson, and that was more charity if anything else.

What if my father was wrong?

What if everything I've ever known was... wrong?

I didn't want to feel that way. Not after everything I've done to get this far. I'd worked hard to finally get my own mission. This had been my one and only chance to prove myself to my father and Elite Humanity. I wanted to help protect humans from the supernaturals who were bad. But now who were the bad guys?

That vampire never stood a chance. When a supernatural commits a crime, they're taken away for punishment, sure, but never death. We were never supposed to kill unless we were caught in the most dire circumstances. Elite Humanity had their own rehabilitation centers for supernaturals who couldn't behave.

Or did they…?

I'd never been to one, but I'd heard the whispers. And yet, what if they were only just that? Whispers. Nothing solid. No proof they exist. I was never told what happened to the supernaturals when they were arrested. I just knew they were taken away in one of our vans to be prosecuted.

What if that was a lie too?

All of these thoughts threatened to suffocate me as I laid in bed, staring at my ceiling. It was the weekend, which meant I didn't have anywhere to be. So I stayed here, wasting the day away while I tried to process everything that had happened the past few weeks; learning my boss was the Lycan King, sleeping with him, the truth about my mother, my father breaking his own rules.

It was too much.

Banging sounded at my front door, yanking me from my thoughts. Frowning, I grabbed my phone, checking the camera. My brother's fist was raised over the door, ready to bang again if he had to. Behind him, Melissa leaned against the corridor wall, looking bored.

My stomach dropped. If they were both here, then that wasn't a good sign. And yet... I couldn't ignore them. They knew I was here or they wouldn't have shown up in the first place.

Groaning, I slipped out of bed, still in my pajamas. Patrick banged on the front door again as I made my way through the living room. I barely had a chance to unlock it before he was shoving his way inside.

"Can I help you?" I asked, arms crossed over my chest.

"You can get dressed," Patrick replied, barely glancing at me. "We're going out. Orders from the top."

The top meaning father.

"What orders?" I frowned, a feeling of uneasiness settling in my ribs. "Where are we going?"

"Get dressed," Melissa cooed, "and we'll tell you."

I had no other choice. They were dressed in black, so I figured I should do the same. Pulling my hunting clothes from the closet, I slipped on the leggings and black t-shirt, complete with the leather jacket. I pulled my hair back into a messy ponytail, knowing it would be better if I was going out with them. Finally, I snagged my dagger from the bedside table, slipping it into its usual sheath at my waist.

They were waiting for me in the living room. Patrick was lounging on my couch, his feet up on the pillows. I shoved them off as I walked by. Melissa though was snooping around my bookshelves, her nose scrunched as if even my choice of literature disgusted her.

"Now will you tell me where we're going?" I asked impatiently, irritated that they liked to just barge into my home whenever they felt like it. As if my personal space was meant for them to invade and judge to their liking.

Patrick smirked, jumping to his feet. Usually when he was like this it was because he was up to no good. Which tended to be often. "You'll see," he replied in an amused tone.

"Oh joy," I mocked, rolling my eyes with fake enthusiasm.

I really fucking hated surprises.

Nonetheless, I followed them out and into the black town car that sat idle in front of my building. I didn't recognize the driver, so he must have been one of theirs. We drove in utter silence with me and Melissa in the back and Patrick in the passenger seat. I tried to ignore their presence, staring at the floor of the car while trying to calm the swirl of anxious butterflies in the pit of my stomach. Wherever they were taking me, I knew it couldn't be good.

I didn't realize where we were going until the car stopped before familiar steel gates.

Bolting upright, I pressed myself into the back of the seat. "Why are we here?" But that was a stupid question. I could piece it together.

"We're here," Patrick said lazily, "to do some research. Because, apparently, Father isn't too happy with your progress."

"He asked you to take me here?" I asked, sweat pricking at my palms.

"Of course." Melissa snorted. "We wouldn't be here otherwise."

This was a terrible idea. "What if he's home?"

"He's not. Our intel is solid," Patrick replied, opening the car door. "Cameras have already been deactivated. The premises are clear."

"The butler?" I was grasping at straws now, looking for any reason not to go in there.

"Taken care of."

I didn't know what that meant and I didn't think I wanted to know. "What if he knows we were here? It'll blow my cover."

"Sweetheart, if we don't find anything tonight, your cover will be the least of your worries." Melissa swung out of the car, slamming the door behind her. Patrick was already up and over the fence, watching as Melissa swung herself up the bars.

I had no choice but to follow.

Feeling sick to my stomach, I climbed the fence after them, my feet hitting the ground with a sharp thud. They were off before I could right myself, taking off toward the house. I trailed behind them, keeping an eye out just in case. I didn't trust that Noah wouldn't just show up while we were in the middle of breaking into his house.

"Best way in?" Melissa asked.

"Back patio." Patrick nodded to the side of the house. We followed his lead, stalking along the side and to the backyard. It looked the same as before when I'd been here a few days ago to have lunch with Noah. The thought of that made my stomach flip.

Melissa knelt by the back door, slipping a key lock pin from her hair. Within a few seconds, the door swung open. Patrick stepped inside, letting his eyes adjust to the dark. We couldn't bring flashlights—even with the lookouts I knew my brother had posted around the property, Noah would see the light from miles away.

So, unfortunately, I was left to face the darkness. Hoping and praying he wouldn't return home. A feeling of guilt and betrayal burned in the pit of my stomach over what we were doing. I didn't understand why I felt the way I did, but I definitely didn't want to be here.

Especially doing this.

It took me a little longer to adjust to the shadows, but it was easy following Melissa's blond hair in the blackness. Ignoring the dining room and kitchen, they made their way towards the stairs.

"Which room is his study?" Patrick asked, glancing over his shoulder.

"To the right," I whispered. It felt weird following them in here, but I couldn't show weakness. I had to do as I was told. Even if I did question everything.

"Good. You take that. Melissa, find his bedroom. I'll search the other rooms." Patrick didn't even wait for us to reply. He took off, bounding up the steps as if we hadn't just broken into a Lycan's house at night.

Numbly, I followed. Turning right at the top of the stairs, my feet led me to the library. I wasn't sure if Noah had replaced the lock that kept his office shut tight, but I was sure I would be able to pick it. Melissa had taught me too well.

The library was pitch black as I slipped inside, the curtains drawn shut over the windows. I felt my way around, remembering the layout from the last time I was here. When my fingers brushed against the solid wood, I knew I'd found the door. Kneeling, I slipped out my own lock pick needle, trying to find the hole in the darkness. It took me a while, but once I found it, it took no time at all to open it.

So he hadn't changed the locks.

Ducking inside, I closed the door behind me. Here, the curtains were open, letting in the moonlight and allowing me to make out his desk and the photos that had stopped me before just behind it. I didn't linger there this time though. Instead, I stayed focused.

No matter how much I didn't want to be here, I had a job to do and the faster I found proof, the faster we would be out of there.

Taking a deep breath, I yanked at the drawers of his desk, surprised to find them unlocked. Then again the office door had been locked so why would he find the need to lock the drawers of his desk? Shaking my head I got to work looking for anything we could use against him, no matter how hard that thought had become.

Rifling through the files and papers there, I strained to read the small print. The first drawer was filled with nothing but legal documents pertaining to his company. I recognized the logo in the right-hand corner immediately. The next was filled with office supplies.

Growing more frustrated, I tried his computer. It flicked on, and I winced at the bright light. When the login screen popped up, I hesitated. I had no idea where to even begin with his password. Turning, I scanned the shelves as if they'd give me a clue. As if there was something there that I could use.

After a moment, a photo caught my eyes and realization settled in me. "Of course." I quickly made my way across the room, picking up one of the photos of Noah and his wife smiling happily in the frame. She was beautiful, far more than I could ever be and though he had them scattered everywhere, I wasn't jealous like most girls would be. Instead, I felt sorry for him. That he had lost the woman he loved more than anything.

With no time to waste I flipped over the photo and read the caption.

Roya & Noah, Laguna Beach 1985

I froze, reading that one line over and over again. Roya. That was his mate's name. A bump in the hall made me jump, reminding me I had precious time I was wasting. Time that could mean life or death. Replacing the photo, I got back to the desk, typing in her name.

And I was in.

Flicking through his documents and files as quickly as I could, I searched for anything that I could use. Until finally, I clicked on his email. At the top, a message from someone that shared the Solvmane name caught my attention. A Shane that I'd never heard about before. I opened it, not knowing what I'd find.

It was a long email thread, spanning months. I scanned the last few, not expecting to find anything about the attacks at all. And boy, was I wrong.

Noah had written to this Shane person—whoever he was—about the recent attacks. My eyes leaped over the words, fingers curling around the mouse tightly. He had no idea who was behind the attacks, but he was trying to figure it out on his own. There was something else in here about another pack out in Australia... one that had to do with Shane.

This was it. This was proof that Noah had nothing to do with the attacks or any secret rebellion. I felt lighter for a moment, unable to stop the grin that tugged at the corners of my lips. Now all I had to do was print it to show Patrick and Melissa. To show my father.

A noise so faint I almost missed it sounded in the library.

I froze, listening hard, hoping it was my brother or sister. Except it wasn't.

It was a window opening, which could only mean one thing.

Someone was home.

SHADOWS IN THE DARKNESS

Noah

We started patrolling that night. After Lawson had given me his full report, I knew I had to do something to try and figure out what Elite Humanity was up to. We had to be careful—I didn't want to repeat what had already happened and lose more of the pack. But we couldn't just sit around and do nothing.

Lawson trailed behind me as we stalked the streets. There were five of us in this group, with more spread out across the city to try and hunt Elite Humanity down. So far, we hadn't had much luck. Either Elite Humanity was being uncharacteristically quiet tonight or they knew we were suspicious of their activity. I really hoped it wasn't the second option—that would mean they really did have an inside man.

"We've been out all night and nothing," Lawson muttered. His fingers curled into fists at his side. I knew what he really wanted, though.

Revenge.

Stopping short, I turned to face the group of men I was with. "We'll call it a night. I want patrols out regularly. Only at night. Keep communication encrypted. I don't want another ambush."

"We're stopping it now?" Lawson whined, eyes flashing with irritation at my call.

"Go home," I ordered. I didn't want him out like this. His need for revenge would cloud his judgment. Besides, we'd been all over our assigned segment of the city and had seen nothing.

Lawson's lip curled, but he didn't argue. Motioning for the others to follow, he turned, heading back to where we'd parked our cars as I trailed after them, keeping my distance. Tonight hadn't gone as I thought it would. I didn't really know what I'd been expecting, but I'd hoped we would have at least been able to find some agents to question.

Reaching our cars, we headed off our separate ways. Lawson hesitating with one hand on the handle. "What do you want us to do when we find them?" he asked quietly.

I studied him. His fingers gripping the handle so tight, that the metal had started to bend. "You won't kill them," I said at last. "Only question them. Is that understood?"

He caught my gaze, fire flickering in his blue eyes. At first, I thought he would fight me on this. Demand justice. But he didn't.

"I understand," he muttered. Without another word, he slipped into his car and started the engine before I watched him tear out of the alley, red lights disappearing around the corner.

I knew he was angry with me about my decision, but I also knew he understood why I ordered it. We needed EH agents alive to question them about the attack. About all of the attacks. I needed to know if they had something to do with the rogue supernaturals killing humans.

Not to mention, I didn't want to go down the same road they were. Killing them wouldn't solve anything. The only thing it would do is start a war that would get more innocent people killed in the crossfire, which was something I couldn't allow.

Getting into my own car, I started for home. Tonight had been a disappointment, but that didn't mean I still couldn't do my own research. I needed to look back at the most recent attacks to see if there was a pattern. Maybe even a zone I could narrow it down to for us to search tomorrow night. There had to be something that would reveal the truth behind all of this.

Something that would give us the answers we needed.

The drive home felt long, the silence weighing heavily on my shoulders. Everything that had happened lately, didn't make sense. But most of all Sydney didn't make sense. There was no denying she had something to do with all of this, no matter how much I didn't want to believe it. The only thing I could do was wait to see what the truth turned out to be. A woman that had turned my mind upside down, and made my cold heart feel things I didn't think possible anymore.

Turning down my street, I sighed heavily trying to focus on the plan ahead instead of the unanswered questions rattling through my brain. Due to the rural location of my home, it was darker out here than it was in the city, the streets completely vacant at this hour but something eerie set the hairs on the back of my neck on edge, my beast growling beneath my skin.

I was distracted. But not distracted enough.

As I stepped out of the car, I paused. The house was dark. Nothing stirred. But something felt off. Hesitating with one hand on the door, I stared up at my house. It looked the same. Quiet. Empty. But sniffing the air, I immediately caught a familiar scent.

Jasmine and roses.

My beast whined, anxiously tugging at the corners of my consciousness. He knew she was here. Or had been. I couldn't be sure. The scent was fresh, still clinging to the air around the drive. Steading my breath, I strained to hear even the slightest of sounds.

At first, there was nothing but the gentle whisper of the wind. And then I heard it.

A scuffle on the second floor. The library. I could hear keys tapping, the sound pinging around in my head. Bristling, I left the car door open. Whoever was in my house was going to regret ever coming here.

I didn't bother to use the front door, they'd hear me. Besides, I didn't need to. My claws snapped out, sharp and ready. Digging into the siding as I hauled myself up, I scaled the side of the house like the predator I was. I was the thing of nightmares, a creature out for blood.

No matter who stood in my way.

The library window was just a few feet above me. I knew I could catch whoever was in my office off guard by taking this route. Slowly, I pulled myself up, lifting the sash. It brushed against the wood, the curtains blowing out into the room from the wind.

Time stood frozen as I hauled myself through the window, crouching beneath it. Nothing moved, nothing seemed to breathe. The door to my office was open, the light of my computer still on. Whoever was in there clearly was looking for something. I wasn't entirely sure what they would be looking for, I had nothing to hide.

Inching forward, I stalked toward the door. There was only one way in and one way out, unless they took a deep dive out the window, which for a human could be a death sentence from the second floor. No matter what, in the end they were trapped. Taking a deep breath, claws ready, I prepared myself for what I was about to do.

However, the moment I stepped around the corner, something flew toward my head. I ducked just in time, rolling to the side. A blur of black sped past me, leaping over the couch before bounding toward the door. I barely had time to collect myself as I raced after it, my beast snarling in the process.

Whatever slipped through the door disappeared into the hall before slamming it shut behind them. Growling, I yanked at the handle, the hinges creaking before breaking off entirely. Tossing the heavy wood to the side, I stormed into the corridor prepared for whatever met me.

The shadow had made it to the stairs. Except now there were three of them. One paused, his face turning slightly to the side, blond hair flashing in the darkness. I recognized him instantly.

"Argent," I snarled.

Patrick smirked, turning to face me. A click resonated through the hall as the safety of the gun in his hand snapped off. Raising it, he aimed for my chest as I leapt forward with only one thing on my mind; death.

Before he could pull the trigger, the smaller shadow yanked his arm down. The shot went wide, burying itself into the carpet. Still, I flinched, my beast whining at the scent of silver in the air. Thoughts of Lawson flashed through my head, but only briefly. The other assailant quickly pushed Patrick toward the stairs, red hair lashing out over their shoulder.

Not their. Her.

Sydney's scent hit me like a storm, wiping anything and everything from my mind. I stood there, frozen, staring as the shadows quickly escaping down the stairs. It wasn't until I heard the front door open and slam shut that I quickly shook myself out of the stupor.

They might have been able to get the upper hand, but they wouldn't escape. Leaping over the banister, the floor shook beneath my feet as I landed in the foyer. I raced out the door, finding my shadows already approaching the gate as they scaled it deftly. Expertly. As if they'd been trained for this.

Which could only mean one thing.

Elite Humanity.

Here. In my house. My beast snarled, begging to be unleashed. I had half a mind to let it go, to allow him to tear them to shreds for what they did to my brother, my people. But something held me back.

I could still smell her. She was everywhere. In my house, in the wind running across my drive. It clung to me, toying with my mind.

Sydney had been here.

The screeching of tires caught my attention, too loud in the silence of the night. I couldn't let them get away. Taking three steps, I launched myself over the car I'd left parked in the drive, the door still open. I was nearly to the gate when the side door of the van flew open. One shadow jumped in, then the other. Patrick's blond hair was unmistakable as he slipped into the back. The last shadow was slower, hesitating with one hand on the handle. She glanced back, but only slightly. I couldn't get a good look at her face.

But that scent...

Someone grabbed her from the inside, hauling her into the van. The door slammed shut and the tires squealed against the pavement. I stopped short, barely breathing as I watched the red tail lights fade into the distance through the bars of the gate. I could just make out a face peeking out the back of the van. But they were too far away, the night just a little too dark for me to make them out.

Or to make her out... to know for sure if it was Sydney...

I couldn't be sure though, whoever that was could have been anyone. The red hair, the scent—it didn't mean that it had been Sydney. Though deep down I knew it was. I just didn't understand why it was so fucking hard for me to accept what she was. Pulling out my phone, I dialed Lawson's number.

"Are we heading back out?" Lawson asked, hope tinging his words when he immediately answered the phone.

"Three EH agents were just at my house," I growled, my eyes glued to the spot where the van had disappeared. "They were looking for something."

"Wait—what?" I could hear him moving on the other end. "I'll be there in ten."

"No, I need you to go somewhere else," I ordered. "Go to Sydney's apartment. Make sure she's there."

"Syd—? Oh, your secretary." Lawson paused for a moment. "Do you think one of those agents was her?" he asked finally.

"I'm not sure. But I will be soon. Just get there as quickly as you can." I ended the call before he could argue. It wouldn't take him long to confirm what I suspected.

Heading back into the house,I closed the door firmly behind me. And then I just stood there. I couldn't shake her scent. It was everywhere. Some of it was old, stale, from the time she'd been here previously. But others... she'd been here. I knew it. I just needed it to be confirmed.

Lawson called back a few minutes later. I answered, my heart dropping. "Yes?"

"She's here, Noah. I'm looking at her right now."

"What's she wearing?" I asked quietly.

"Looks like pajamas to me. T-shirt and shorts."

I ended the call.

Lawson had seen her in her apartment. But that didn't mean she hadn't been here tonight. It didn't mean she wasn't working for Elite Humanity.

And if that were true... then she owed me an explanation.

THE EYES THAT WATCH ME

SYDNEY

Tonight hadn't gone as I had expected, though, what was I to expect? We had broken into his home and the move, though completely idiotic, did serve its purpose. However, the moment I saw him standing there, I couldn't breathe. Every part of me screamed that this had been wrong.

The second I made it back to my apartment and slammed the door shut behind me, I gasped for air. I hadn't realized I had been holding my breath until I leaned against the sturdy wood, trying to catch it. I knew it had been a bad idea to go with my brother and sister tonight, but they'd made it seem as if I wasn't allowed to say no. Besides, I didn't think they'd do something crazy.

Like breaking into the Lycan King's own home crazy.

It had been insane to even think we could pull that off. Patrick and Melissa were extremely good at what they did, but not that good. We'd high-tailed it out of there, driving like madmen through the streets of New York. I was surprised we hadn't been pulled over with the way one of Patrick's men had been driving.

The images of him standing in his driveway watching us go forever imprinted in my mind.

They'd dropped me off first, which I didn't mind. I was done with tonight as it was. I wasn't about to stick around to find out what else they'd get up to that night. Besides, I had what I needed. Just before Noah had slunk through the window, I forwarded his email to Shane to my own Elite Humanity one before destroying the evidence with one of our bugs. He would never know. But my father would.

For a brief second, I allowed myself to feel some sort of pride in what I had done tonight. My only mission was to find evidence about the attacks and, in a way, I had. I had proof that Noah wasn't behind this. At least, some type of proof. The email looked personal, and it had probably been sent to another Lycan or shifter, so Noah had no reason to lie about his lack of involvement with what was going on. I was sure EH would be able to look up whoever this Shane person was and verify that.

So, I'd completed my mission.

Successfully.

Grinning, I pushed off the door, stretching my arms over my head. Tonight was a pretty good workout. Either that or I'd been out of training for far too long. To be fair, we scaled a steel fence twice and ran away from the king of all Lycans. It had been a close call, but we'd still gotten away.

Or, at least I think we did.

There was no doubt that Noah would know it had been Elite Humanity that had broken into his house. He'd recognized Patrick easily enough.

The smile slipped from my lips. Had he recognized me as well? I wasn't so sure and dread began to pool in the pit of my stomach. I shouldn't have cared. My job was done, after all. I probably wouldn't even be returning to work on Monday, anyway. But I couldn't help but feel a little... sad about it. Frightened even.

What if he tracked me down? What if he came after us for revenge? He was probably already looking for the people responsible for his brother's injuries and, if he recognized Patrick, he would connect the dots eventually. Shaking my head, I started for the bedroom. I needed to get out of these clothes, and a nice, long shower would be just the thing to distract me.

First, I checked my phone left on the nightstand, clicking on my email. Feeling relieved the forwarded message was still in my inbox, I made sure to forward it again. Just in case. I couldn't lose the only evidence I'd found in weeks. Not when my father's patience was already running thin. Placing the phone back on the table, I went straight to the bathroom.

Stripping out of the black leggings, top, and jacket felt like shedding a second skin—one I didn't like staying in too long. Tossing them into the hamper, I buried them beneath the other clothes just so I wouldn't have to see them when I passed by again. I took my time in the shower, letting the hot water relax my tense muscles, trying not to think about Noah or the attacks or anything else, really. All I wanted to do was get all of this over with and move on to the next mission.

Because that was my job. My purpose.

Before that would have motivated me. Made me feel empowered. Now, I just felt drained.

Grabbing my favorite lounge-wear; a pair of the softest shorts ever invented and a plain, soft tee, I pulled them on, sighing with satisfaction at how they felt. The clean, comfy clothes made me feel just a little better—but that was better than sinking into the dark feelings I knew crouched at the corners of my mind.

Walking out of the bathroom, I only half-attempt to dry my hair with a towel, scrunching it from the bottom to keep my curls from looking like an absolute mess the next day. Before distractedly, I wandered into the living room, aiming for the kitchen. I was halfway there when I heard the telltale sign of my alarm system going off.

I froze, staring at my front door, praying it wasn't my siblings. Or worse... Noah. There was no way in hell he'd gotten here so fast, and I knew for a fact my brother and sister were probably heading straight to father to report back to him. Which meant I had no idea who was currently lurking outside.

If they even were outside my door.

I'd rigged my apartment from all angles; from the roof to the windows. I couldn't tell which alarm had been tripped, but I could find out. I inched toward my door, flipping open the black pad. Inside, a single small light blinked next to a hastily written note.

The roof.

Without thinking, I glanced up nervously. Patrick and Melissa wouldn't bother with trying to sneak in. That wasn't their style. Had Noah sent someone to check if I was home? If he'd suspected that I'd been there tonight, that could very well be the case.

I try to calm my heart rate, taking deep breaths as I back away from the door. If someone was trying to check in on me, and they happened to be supernatural, it would be easy enough for them to scale the side and look through the windows. I wrapped the towel around my hair, hiding my face as I checked the living room ones, but I could see only the lights of the city, cutting through the darkness of the night and nothing else.

I forced myself to walk slowly to the fridge, open it, and check what was inside, though my mind was nowhere near wondering what was for dinner tonight. Instead, I closed the door to the fridge and pressed the button for the electric kettle that sat on the counter near it as if I was about to make myself some tea. The alarm clicked off as the apartment went silent.

Stop being paranoid, I thought, shaking my head. *It could just be a pigeon.*

Seemed unlikely, but it helped lower my heart rate enough for me to finally breathe. While grabbing a cup from the cupboard, I felt the hair on the back of my neck start to rise. As if someone was watching me. Instead of reacting, I continued the farce, dumping a tea bag into the cup before pouring the hot water over it. Taking my sweet time stirring the contents, I left my eyes and ears wide open, just in case I wasn't being paranoid.

It was too quiet now. Nothing stirred. I could faintly hear the usual sounds of a New York night outside my windows, but I was so far up they were faint. The sound of my own breathing was louder, shaky and unstable in my ears as I tried to pretend everything was normal. I strained to hear any telltale signs of someone up on the roof, or scaling the walls to get to my windows. But I heard nothing.

Instead my phone rang in the next room, causing me to jump. My tea nearly ended up on the floor, the liquid trembling as I furiously berated myself for reacting. I was a trained professional, and I really needed to act like one. Setting the cup on the counter, I darted into my bedroom, reaching my phone just in time.

"Hello?" I hadn't checked the caller ID.

"Where the hell are you?" I could hear the barely controlled fury in Noah's voice.

Ice spread through my veins. "At home, why?" My voice didn't shake, but my hand was.

There was nothing but silence on the other end and, for a moment, I thought he'd just hung up.

"Nothing." He cleared his throat. "I'll see you on Monday." The line went dead.

I let out a shaky breath, sitting down heavily on the mattress. If he was calling me this late—and for no good reason—then he must have suspected me. Which meant he'd definitely sent someone to check in on me as well. I'd gotten lucky tonight, having enough time to get in the shower and make it seem like I'd been here all along without even trying. Really damn lucky.

My phone vibrated, and I flipped the screen over to read the message.

Your siblings found proof that the King is leading them. Report to headquarters for a debriefing immediately.

I frowned, rereading the message over and over until the words burned into my mind. That couldn't be right. Neither Patrick nor Melissa had said anything about finding evidence on the drive back. Sure, we might have been a little distracted in escaping a Lycan but knowing them, they would have been boasting about it the minute we were safe. The fact that they hadn't...

And then there was *my* evidence. According to the emails, Noah was innocent. He had about as much of an idea as to who was behind the attacks as we did. And that was from his own personal computer. How had Melissa or Patrick found anything that could link Noah to the attacks? And where did they even find that?

Something wasn't right. I could feel it tugging at the back of my mind. There was a slim possibility that we'd found conflicting evidence, but I doubted it. Mine was solid enough. Noah had no reason to lie—not in his private messages to someone he was clearly close to.

Unless he did.

Confusion twisted in my gut, tearing me in two. Maybe I was mistaken. Maybe I just hoped he wasn't involved. Whatever feelings I'd started to have toward him could very well be getting in the way of my duty. Patrick and Melissa knew what they were doing—they'd been in the field far longer than I have. They had more experience. Whatever they'd found had to be damning enough to convince my father.

I didn't know who was right—me or my siblings. But I knew there was only one way to find out.

I guess I was heading home.

CLAIMING WHAT'S MINE

NOAH

Monday morning finally arrived.

And Sydney never showed up.

I waited for her inside my office, waiting to hear the sound of her footsteps coming down the corridor. For the scent of jasmine and rose to fill the hallway and linger in my office. But it never came. When an hour had passed, I finally pushed away from my desk, stalking out into the hall. Mr. Grey was coming down from the opposite side, his footsteps nearly silent.

"Where is Sydney?" I asked, not bothering with niceties this morning.

"She's called in sick, sir," Grey replied coldly. He didn't seem surprised. "You know how frail these humans can be," he added.

I didn't know if I believed that excuse, and the suspicion that had slowly been burning through me all weekend flared up once again. Yet, after so many days, I can't tell if the scent I'd caught had really been hers or a part of my own subconsciousness. I hadn't told Lawson what I'd found that night, only that I knew they were from Elite Humanity and one of them had been Patrick Argent.

We knew Laurent had three children, though no one knew much about the youngest one. Apparently, they weren't old enough to be in the field just yet. Their older brother and sister, however, were a different story. I knew more about Patrick than I did Melissa, but they were both on my radar.

"Did you find anything I asked about last week?" I asked him, recalling the phone conversation I had with him about getting intel on Sydney.

He stared at me for a moment before shaking his head, "no I didn't. Which is odd because I'm usually able to. I was going to try to visit in person but I wanted to clear that with you first."

I could have him do that, go to see her in person. Use his skills to uncover the truth, but what good would that do if she really wasn't what I had expected her to be.

"No," I replied after a moment. "I'll deal with it myself."

Heading back into my office, I pulled out my phone. Clicking on Sydney's contact, I tried to call her.

Straight to voicemail.

With a frustrated growl, I shoved it back into my pocket and took a seat. I tried to focus on my actual work, but I was too distracted. It was too quiet up here with just me and Grey. Too empty. My mind continuously wandered back to the night she came with me to dinner, to the night Elite Humanity had broken into my own house. I couldn't have imagined her scent. I wasn't that far gone, was I?

That uncomfortable thought stuck with me for the rest of the day. I left early, knowing I wasn't going to be able to do much being this distracted. A part of me hoped that, if I just went home and returned the next morning, she would be here.

But she wasn't.

Nor did she come in the next day after that, either.

It didn't matter how many times I called or emailed, if I threatened to fire her or demand that she return to work, it all went straight to voicemail or completely unanswered. I heard nothing for days. I'd even sent Lawson back to her apartment to check on her, yet she wasn't there. It was almost as if she'd just disappeared entirely.

By the fourth day, I'd started to worry. My beast had been anxious all week, practically begging for us to go check on her, to make sure she was safe or if she was still alive. I'd been fighting him constantly, knowing I had no right to do that. No reason. Yet the longer I stayed away, the angrier I became.

She had no right to disappear on me like that. No right to forgo her contract and ignore my calls. The anger was like a festering blister, growing more and more toxic by the day. It was a feeling so intense, I didn't know what to do with it. Each night I distracted myself by running the patrols, but that didn't help either. Elite Humanity had gone just as silent as Sydney had.

Which didn't help in assuaging my suspicion. If anything, it made me more and more sure that I had caught her scent in my house that night.

Finally, on the fifth day, I'd had enough. Instead of heading to work, I turned toward her apartment complex, weaving between traffic that was dangerously close to being illegal. But I didn't care. If she wasn't going to come to work, then I was going to her. There was nowhere else she could have gone. I'd already done a background check on her. She had no family in the area, no family at all. According to state records, her parents had already passed, and she was entirely alone. Which meant she had to be home at some point, and I would wait outside her door all day and night if I had to.

I parked in the garage beneath her complex, barely bothering to lock the doors as I stormed toward the elevator. It went agonizingly slow as I made my ascent to the penthouse. As soon as the doors opened, I stalked down the hall toward her door. My fist banging against the wood, my anger just barely controlled as I waited to hear anything from the other side.

At first, I heard nothing. I almost believed she wasn't home until I heard the telltale sign of a breath catching beyond the wood.

Sydney.

"Open up," I barked. "I know you're in there."

There was a moment of hesitation before I heard the locks click open. The door cracked just a little, barely enough for me to see one green eye blink into view.

"What are you doing here?" Sydney asked, sounding wary but not surprised.

"Open the door," I repeated, leaving no room for her to disobey.

Still, she stood there, refusing to budge. "Go away, Noah." She sounded tired. As if that spark I'd always seen in her had dimmed.

As the door started to close, I stopped it with one hand, barely having to use any strength at all to peel it open. Sydney stepped back, eyes going wide as I stepped inside.

"Get out." Now there was that anger. That spark. She glared up at me, hands curling into fists at her side. She was still as beautiful as the day she walked into my office, and though I was completely pissed about her lack of communication, every bit of my anger slowly fizzled away with the desire to claim her growing stronger by the second.

"No," I replied, glancing around the spacious room, trying to find any reason for her to be here rather than at work where she should have been.

Her arms crossed over her chest. "I'll call the cops."

"Go right ahead, Princess." I chuckled, closing the door behind me with one foot, as I leaned against the wood, mirroring her stance. Her eyes flicked toward my arms as they laced over my chest.

She didn't move. Instead, she fled.

I caught her halfway across the living room, my arm snaking around her waist until her back was firmly against my chest. She writhed in my arms, trying to twist out of my grip, but I refused to let go. Her pulse raced beneath her skin, her heartbeat pounding in my ears.

Brushing my lips against her cheek, I whispered. "Come back to me."

Sydney stopped struggling, chest rising and falling with each heavy breath. "Fuck you," she breathed.

I have no idea what it was I'd done, but her fire raced through me, igniting my own. "Turn around."

She hesitated. I felt every small change in her body; from the way her thighs clenched together to the soft sound of a gasp escaping from her lips. My pulse quickened at the sharp scent in the air. Still, she didn't move.

"Turn around," I repeated slowly, my voice dangerously low.

"No," she finally replied. "Let me go and get out of my house."

Was she being serious?

"You say that, but something tells me that isn't what you really want. Now tell me what you are avoiding me." I wanted to know, I had to know what the hell was going on and why she was acting as if she feared me. I had spent so much time with her and never once had she fled from me or acted as if she couldn't be in my presence. At least not that I recalled.

She was quiet for a moment before a scoff left her throat, "you are so sure of yourself aren't you? Nothing about you makes me want you here."

Ouch. The blow wasn't something I was expecting, but I knew damn well she was lying.

Anger sparked in my chest, my hand slipping lower across her stomach, still pinning her in place. "If I place my hand between your thighs right now, how hot and wet would you feel?" I wondered aloud.

Sydney leaned back into me, eyes going wide as my other hand trailed along her spine, fingers tangling in that wild hair of hers until she was forced to look back at me. I caught those green eyes with my own as she breathed out heavily, trying to avoid my gaze.

"Did you forget?" I murmured, my breath hot against her neck. "You're mine. We have a contract, Sydney. One that I haven't released you from just yet."

"You don't own me," Sydney argued, but it came out in barely a whisper. Her lips trembled slightly, as her eyes flicked between my eyes and my lips.

My anger turned to fury. This puny, weak human girl had a way of igniting my beast like no one else. "But I do. I own you, and I want nothing more than to prove that to you."

Spinning her around, my hands lifted her by the waist until her thighs were wrapped around me. Her breath hitched, nails digging into my chest as she tried to pull away. But her attempt was weak. I could see the truth in her eyes, how badly she wanted this. Her tongue flicked out, wetting her lower lip as I stalked toward the bedroom.

I didn't realize just how much anger could feel like lust until just now.

All I wanted to do was take what was mine.

My hands tore at the leggings clinging to her skin, peeling them off one leg at a time before wrapping them back around me. Her shirt was next, tugged over her head and tossed to the floor as my lips found her neck. My teeth grazed her skin, nipping at the sensitive spots until I heard her gasp in my ear.

Her nails dug into my shoulders as I released myself from my own clothes. I'd thought about how I would take her again, allowing myself one small guilty pleasure. But now that I was here, now that we were back to where we started, I couldn't remember what I'd planned. All I wanted—all I needed—was to slam myself inside her tight pussy and bury myself deep inside her.

"Tell me you want this," I mumbled against her neck. "Say yes..."

She was hesitant for a moment, her breath coming in and out rapidly as I slid my hand up her thigh towards her core, causing her back to arch until finally, she replied.

"Yes..."

In one swift movement, I took what had always been mine. Her pussy was hot and eager for my cock, convulsing around me as she adjusted to the girth. Her head tilted back, soft moans slipping from her lips. I caught them with my own, swallowing her desire as her nails raked down my chest.

The sweet smell of her arousal was stronger now, wiping everything from my mind. I could faintly hear the sounds of our bodies coming together, but it didn't register. All I could feel was her pussy tightening around me, the soft, strangled cries and tortured moans as I ravaged her.

And yet, I still needed more.

Gritting my teeth, I pistoned up into her, slamming my entire length into her welcoming heat. She cried out once, then twice, as if she could barely hold back her pleasure. I wanted to hear her beg for it. I wanted to hear my name on her lips.

"Noah," she moaned, reading my mind.

And that one word had me coming undone. I pinned her to my chest, thrusting up one final time. Her body tensed, shivers rolling down her spine as she cried out again before going limp in my arms. My teeth lengthened as my beast fought to break free, my mind clouded by lust as I bit down into her neck, allowing myself to release everything I'd been holding back.

And, in that moment, I knew I was completely and royally fucked.

STING OF BETRAYAL

SYDNEY

The fading memories of pleasure rolled through me as I slowly awoke. I knew I was in my room, the familiar walls greeting me as I opened my eyes. It's my room, alright, but something felt different. Shifting slightly, I felt a weight over my waist. And then everything came rushing back.

Noah had shown up at my doorstep, forcing his way inside despite my weak attempts at protesting. He'd picked me up as if I weighed nothing, lighting the fire of desire within me. That fire had torn through us both as we had sex over and over. Just when I'd thought he was done, he'd pull me closer and start it all over again. This morning, I felt the repercussions of that. My body was exhausted but in a good way.

Neither of us were fully naked. He'd helped me into my comfy clothes last night as my legs shook too much to hold me up. He'd put on his boxer-briefs, keeping his chest bare. As we curled up last night in my bed, I couldn't help but feel happy.

The feeling of him moving behind me now, turning onto his back caused me to freeze for a moment before I rolled over, my eyes tracing every exposed curve of his body. They caught on to the faint red lines that criss-crossed his shoulders, his spine. My breath caught, hand reaching up before I could think about what I was doing. My fingers trailing over the scars lightly as I barely touched him. Causing a soft growl to emit from his throat.

So you are awake? I guess it's time for the awkward shit.

"What happened?" I whispered, worried I was crossing a line.

He was silent, his face turned away from me. Even after last night, even after chasing me down, he was still guarded. Closed off. Frustration built in my chest. My fingers slowed before stopping entirely.

"I know."

His back muscles rippled uneasily. "Know what?" There was a guarded tone to his voice.

I decided to just go for it. "That you're not human."

Noah stilled, becoming like stone. Just when I thought he wasn't going to reply, he murmured, "Is that so? And how do you know that?"

Now it was me who couldn't answer. Because what would I say? That I'd always known supernaturals existed? That, actually, I'd been trained to take them down my entire life? That I was a part of Elite Humanity, one of his greatest enemies?

I couldn't say any of that. Not if I still wanted to live. I didn't know how he'd react to the truth. He would know it was me who had helped break into his house the other night, that I was part of the organization that had nearly killed his brother. Probably killed his mate. He'd want revenge. He'd kill me then.

"When I was younger, I saw something I shouldn't have," I lied, the words tasting too sour on my lips. "Since then, I've always known they existed."

He finally turned to face me, blue eyes wary. "And?"

"And what?" I pulled the blanket around my shoulders, shielding myself.

"Are you frightened?"

I took a minute to think over my answer. "No," I said finally. "Not with you." That at least was the truth. I didn't feel like Noah was the monster hiding in the shadows. I truly didn't feel like he wanted to hurt me. But that was probably because he didn't know the truth.

His hand reached up, fingers trailing along my cheek. "So you know what I am."

It wasn't a question, but I felt I had to answer anyway. "Yes."

"And you're not scared."

"No."

Something flickered in his eyes then—hope, maybe? I couldn't tell.

"What am I to you?" The words were out of my mouth before I could stop them. I had no reason to ask that question. All we've ever done was have sex. But it didn't feel like just sex to me. I couldn't ignore the feelings that had been slowly burning through me for the past few weeks. I wanted him.

If he would have me.

Noah's jaw flexed. "I—I don't know."

But I could tell that was a lie. The way he looked at me now was like I was all he'd ever wanted. I could feel his heart beating steadily in his chest, the warmth of his body pressed against mine. This wasn't just sex to him either. I knew that deep in my bones.

"Sydney, I—"

There was a loud crack, like wood splintering. We were both on our feet in an instant, my knife already in my hands, his claws already out. We glanced at each other, our eyes catching on our weapons before meeting again. But there was no time.

Before I could react, my bedroom door was thrown open. Elite Humanity agents streamed into my room, guns raised and pointed toward Noah. I froze, only able to watch as they surrounded him. Noah snarled, swiping at the closest agent.

"I wouldn't do that if I were you," a familiar voice called. Whipping around, I found Patrick's gun pointed toward my head.

Noah froze immediately, pain lashing across his face. The agents wasted no time. Silver chains were clamped around his wrists, his neck. The scent of burning skin filled the room, making me sick to my stomach. Noah's breath hissed out in pain, his body tensing as he tried to withstand the poisonous metal. His claws retracted, skin turning red from where the silver touched his skin.

"Not so high and mighty now, are we?" Patrick asked, smirking. I'd never hated my brother more in that moment. Loathing burned through me, my mind going blank with rage. "I guess you were good for something, sister."

"Sister?" Noah's voice was weaker now.

Any fight I had in me disappeared. I couldn't look at him, couldn't see the look of betrayal I knew was on his face right now. I could feel his anger and disbelief even from across the room. I didn't need to see it to know what I'd just done.

"You didn't know?" Patrick mocked in surprise. "And here I thought you were some untouchable beast that knew everything."

"Oh, brother, you overestimated him." Melissa stepped into the room, looking downright gleeful. Her eyes trailed over Noah's body appreciatively. "At least she had a good-looking specimen."

Guilt and shame ripped through me. Not because of what I'd done with Noah but because of what I know I've just done to him. I heard a slight thump as his knees hit the floor, the pain becoming too much for even him. The other agents barely reacted, their guns still aimed at his heart.

"Patrick, let him go." I sounded far braver than I felt at that moment. "He has nothing to do with the attacks. I have proof of it."

"Unfortunately, so do we. And it is anything but innocent." Patrick sneered, the safety of his gun clicking off. He glanced over at Noah. "If you want her to live, you better get up, beast. Start walking."

"You'd really... kill... your own sister?" Noah spat out. He still wouldn't look at me, no matter how much my eyes begged him to.

"Do you really want to test me?" Patrick replied, cocking the gun.

Noah's head bowed. A second passed, then another. At first, I didn't think he was even able to get up from the floor with the amount of silver on him, but then he slowly rose. His lips were thinned, pain etched into every line on his face. One agent shoved him forward, unable to wait for him to gather his strength enough to walk. Noah stumbled, catching himself at the edge of my bed.

"Noah..." My voice was barely a whisper, too afraid to say his name any louder.

His shoulders tensed, eyes flicking up to meet mine briefly. All I could see was betrayal. Heartbreak. And then it was gone, replaced with nothingness. His eyes went blank, hiding any and all emotion from me. I could practically feel the wall go up, cementing in place, creating a crater between us.

"I'm sorry. Noah, I'm—"

He turned his face away as he slowly walked toward the bedroom door. The Elite Humanity agents trailed after him, their guns never leaving his body. Tears pricked at my eyes, knowing that whatever had been between us was now broken. Maybe forever.

I didn't even know if I'd ever see him again.

Panic replaced the feeling of loss at the thought of that. Before, I would think that he would just be sent off to one of the rehabilitation centers for questioning. But after going hunting with my father, I knew Elite Humanity wasn't playing by the rules they'd created so long ago. And the look on my brother's face…

"Patrick, please." I turned to him, begging. "Let me prove to you. I have it right here." I turned, grabbing my phone from the bedside table.

Patrick's lip curled as he looked down at me. Taking my phone, he dropped it to the floor, crushing it beneath one booted heel. I heard the sound of glass cracking as my screen went dark.

"We don't need your proof," he spat. "As far as Father's concerned, you've failed. You were to report home this week and yet you didn't. I can't help but wonder why. How angry do you think he is right about now?"

I swallowed my fear, my heart caught in my throat. This felt like a setup, yet he was right at the same time. I hadn't reported to Father just yet because I wasn't sure if he would have believed me. And I didn't want to go home without actual proof that would surpass my siblings' to show that Noah was innocent. That's what I'd been doing the past few days—sneaking into his house while he was at work to go through his things. But I'd found nothing.

Which should have been proof enough.

But now I realized, it never would have been enough.

My head whipped up as I stared daggers at my brother and sister. "You used me."

"And you made it too easy, little sister," Melissa replied, a coy smile on her face. "However, we should give her some credit. Thanks to her, we now have the King of the Lycans in our possession. Father will be pleased." She paused, head tilting to the side. "At least with us."

With one last gloating look, Patrick clicked the safety back on his gun before leaving the room. Melissa trailed after him, her nails dragging across the wood of my door before she too disappeared. All I could do was stand there, frozen. I knew I should go after them, knew I should be doing something to try and stop them.

But what could I do? I was just one girl, one human.

There was only one person who would be able to help.

I just hoped he wouldn't kill me before I had a chance to explain.

SEEKING HELP

SYDNEY

I yanked on a sweatshirt and leggings, throwing my hair back into a ponytail and slipped my lock pin into my pocket as I raced out the door. I knew where they were taking Noah. There was only one place he could go, straight to my father at headquarters. But there was nothing I could do for him on my own. I needed help.

There was only one person I knew who might listen to me, though he could very well just kill me, too. I hoped he wouldn't. I hoped he'd give me the chance to explain, to see reason. Because if he didn't, then Noah would die. And I couldn't let that happen.

The only problem with my plan was that I had no idea how to find Noah's brother.

I need to find Lawson.

Darting out of the elevator as soon as the doors opened, I unlocked the town car before slipping inside. I tore out of the parking garage like hell hounds were on my heels, darting between traffic as I headed toward the one place I knew might be a good place to start.

The entire drive to Noah's house, all I could think about was what my family might be doing to him. I'd seen the chains burning his skin, remembered the scent of burning in the air as they forced him from my apartment. It would take them a few hours to reach headquarters, but it would take me longer. Especially when I had to find an errant Lycan that I knew absolutely nothing about.

As soon as I hit the highway, I took off. I wove through the New York traffic desperately, my hands gripped the wheel until my knuckles turned white. I knew I had no time to waste. My heart was in my throat, nearly suffocating me as I raced toward Noah's home. It was a long shot, but it was the only place I knew where I had a chance of finding his brother. If he wasn't there, I had no clue what I would do.

If I didn't find Lawson Solvmane, then I would go to head-quarters on my own. I knew my father would have me killed for disobeying him, for betraying Elite Humanity, but I didn't care. I couldn't let Noah die. Especially not when it was my fault that he'd been caught in the first place.

My father had set me up. I realized that now. I'm not sure if he knew what would happen when he sent me into Noah's company, but looking back, I now knew he'd probably hoped I'd become Noah's weakness. The comments from my sister, learning about our mother, were all carefully placed suggestions I had overlooked. They'd wanted me to get close to Noah so they could easily get to him.

I'd been the bait the entire time.

By the time I screeched to a stop outside the steel gates, I was a mess. Throwing the door open, I took a running leap, clambering over the fence. My feet hit the drive, and I was off again. I didn't stop until my knuckles met the front door, banging until I finally heard footsteps on the other side.

The butler appeared, looking a little worse for wear, but seemed alright. I didn't know what my brother had done to get him out of the house when we broke in, but it didn't seem like he'd gone easy. The butler's eye was still black and swollen with a cut on his upper lip that hadn't healed yet. He'd looked old before, but now he seemed to have aged another decade.

"Can I help you?" he asked stiffly. "Mr. Solvmane isn't here."

"Noah's brother. Where is he?" I was panting now, trying to catch my breath even when I felt I couldn't breathe.

"I'm not sure—"

"It's an emergency. I need to get a hold of him," I ordered. "Now."

The butler's eyes widened slightly. He opened the door, letting me in. "Just a moment."

As I stepped into the foyer, he disappeared upstairs. I waited anxiously, pacing back and forth before the door. The seconds ticked by, our time running out. Finally, Lawson appeared at the top of the stairs. I knew who he was from my briefing when I'd first been assigned to this mission. He seemed healed, with no evidence of the silver that had ravaged his body just a few days ago. The similarities between him and Noah were so startling that I hesitated, pain lashing through me.

"Why are you here?" he asked, gripping the banister. "Where's Noah?"

"They took him."

There was a brief, tense pause. "Who took him?"

"Elite Humanity. I know you know who they are. They took Noah and I need your help."

Another short silence. He stood frozen at the top of the stairs, those piercing blue eyes narrowing. Before I could register any movement, he had me pinned to the front door, his hand around my throat. I gasped, trying to draw air as his fingers squeezed the life from my lungs.

"So you were working with them," he snarled, baring his canines. "I should kill you."

I had about two seconds before he would rip my throat out. My hands went up as I tried to get the words out. "I'm… trying to… help."

"Lawson," the butler hissed, appearing at the top of the stairs. "Let her speak."

Lawson growled a warning, refusing to release me. Black spots appeared at the edge of my vision, sparking across my eyes. I could feel my energy draining as the shadows began to take over. My words were choked off, turning to desperate gulps of what little air I could breathe in.

"Lawson."

He still didn't let go. I could feel his claws digging into my neck, breaking the skin. Heat slowly trickled down my throat, the metallic scent of blood in the air. I was losing too much oxygen, my head going light and fuzzy. Finally, he dropped me. My knees hit the floor as I gasped. The shadows slowly receded, though the world tilted slightly as I tried to gain my composure. My pulse fluttered in my throat, my head pounding.

"You have five seconds to explain," Lawson spat.

"We don't have the time," I gasped, one hand rubbing my throat. I slowly stood, using the door to prop me up. "They took him. We have to save him."

"What do you mean, they took him?" Lawson's eyes flashed.

"Noah was at my house. They just barged in and took him," I replied impatiently. "I don't have time to explain. I need your help. That's why I came here."

"And you just stood by and watched them?" Lawson snarled, taking a step closer. He towered over me, fingers curling and uncurling at his sides. "How can I trust you? This could be a trap."

"It's not a trap. I need your help," I pleaded. "We have to go to EH headquarters and—"

He scoffed, turning away. "I'm not going anywhere with you."

Anger flicked through me. "So what's your plan, then? To just barge into headquarters, fangs bared? You'd be dead in seconds. You need me just as much as I need you."

Lawson whipped around, teeth flashing. "I don't need you."

"You do if you want to have both of you come out of this alive," I shot back. "Don't be stupid. You won't make it two seconds in there without me."

"And how do you know so much?" Lawson's voice dropped, deadly calm. "How do you know you'll be able to get us in and out alive?"

"Because I know that place like the back of my hand," I told him. "Because I grew up there my entire life. I know everything about Elite Humanity, which is why I know we need to stop wasting time and leave. Right now."

I could practically see the wheels turning in Lawson's head. His eyes narrowed, studying me closely. "You're Laurent's third kid."

"So what if I am?" I crossed my arms.

Lawson scoffed. "And you want me to trust you? There's no way in hell." He reached around me, gripping the door handle.

I planted myself firmly in front of the door, refusing to budge. "You're going to have to trust me. For Noah's sake."

"Give me one good reason," Lawson hissed.

I met his gaze, fire meeting fire. Every feeling I'd been trying to repress the past few weeks bubbled up. Images of Noah flicked through my mind; the first time I'd met him, the night we went to dinner, the feeling of his arms wrapped around me as we slept. It all came crashing down, washing over me like a wave that threatened to drown me.

I hadn't known when I'd met him that this would turn out to be anything more than a mission. He was the enemy. A monster. Everything I had been taught to hate. And yet I couldn't deny the feelings I felt now. Couldn't ignore what he did to me. The very thought of losing him tore into me like a silver blade, twisting in my heart.

"Because," I whispered, "I love him."

Lawson's eyes searched mine, trying to find the lie. But I knew he would only see the truth. Because it was true. Somewhere between then and now, I'd fallen for Noah. It didn't matter what he was, what I was. All that mattered was that I knew I wouldn't be able to live without him.

Lawson's lip curled. "If you're lying to me..."

"I'm not."

He leaned in closer, his face just inches away from mine. "If you are," he said again, growling, "then I'll rip you to pieces."

Lawson shoved me aside, throwing the front door open. I caught myself just in time before I hit the ground again. He stopped in the doorway, glancing over his shoulder with a look of death in his eyes. "You better get your shit together," he said. "Because we're leaving. Now."

He stalked down the stairs toward the garage. Without looking back, I followed. I wasn't sure what my plan was. I hadn't had the time to figure it out. But with my knowledge of Elite Humanity's headquarters, and a Lycan on my side, I didn't think it would be too hard to get to Noah.

I just really hoped we wouldn't die in the process.

PRISONER

Noah

The silver-plated chair they had me chained to burned my skin. More chains were wrapped around my wrist, ankles, and neck, making it nearly impossible to move. Pain lanced through me, an endless wave of torture as I sat there in that blank room awaiting my death. Elite Humanity had dragged me here from the van they'd taken me in, my body too weak from the silver to be able to move on its own. All I could do was allow them to treat me how they wanted.

The room was bare with only one door at the far end. The walls were plain cement, matching the ceiling and the floor. Clearly, Elite Humanity had little patience for decorating. It was a classic interrogation room, with a two-way mirror taking up the left wall. The air felt too hot, though that could have just been due to the fact my skin was currently burning from the silver.

My head lolled to the side, my vision tinged with black as I fought to stay conscious. Not that I cared. Sydney's betrayal had broken something inside me. I had no fight left. No willingness to even try to escape. Because what was the point? My beast had gone quiet, broken, and mourning.

The only other person in the room was Patrick. He paced before me, agitated. He'd been interrogating me for the past hour, though there wasn't much I could give him. Over and over, he asked the same question, gripping the stun wand in his hand. Usually, it would have little to no effect on me. But I was weak, the silver burning into my skin. Each time I'd give an answer he didn't like, he'd stick me, the electricity jolting through my body.

"How many supernaturals are you leading in this little rebellion?" Patrick asked again for what seemed like the hundredth time.

"I told you..." My voice was weak, laced with pain. "I'm not leading any rebellion, you idiot."

My head snapped to the side, cheek stinging from the right hook Patrick had landed. If I'd been unchained, he never would have been able to lay a hand on me. The fucking coward. The jolt of electricity came next, the tip of the wand digging into my chest. I bit back the pain, gritting my teeth until I thought they would break.

"We know you're revolting against Elite Humanity," Patrick hissed, leaning forward, his hands resting on the chair's arms. I could see the hatred in his eyes, feel the loathing rolling from him in waves. "You think you're better?" he growled. "You think you deserve to rule this world? That you deserve the power?"

He has no idea how the power thing actually works. Not that I'd tell him, fucking idiot.

I raised my head, meeting his gaze. "I think you and your entire family are insane," I spat. Blood flecked the cement floors. "I'm not leading a rebellion," I repeated slowly. "If anything, I help keep the supernaturals in line. If you kill me, what do you think they'll do? What do you think my pack will do?"

Patrick scoffed, turning away. "We're not afraid of your little pack," he replied, sounding amused. "We have plans to get rid of them anyway—anyone who has aided you in this little plot will be taken down."

"So that was your plan." I tried to keep my head up but failed. I was too weak, the silver draining my strength. "You needed an excuse to finally wipe us all out."

"We never needed an excuse," Patrick snarled. "We kept you monsters alive out of mercy."

Now it was my turn to scoff. "Mercy. You've got to be kidding me. You know nothing about mercy. You're just the well-behaved dog your father beat into submission."

Patrick lunged forward, gripping the chain around my neck and yanking me forward. "You're the only dog here," he hissed. "And I'll be sure to put you down like one, too."

"Enough." Laurent's voice echoed around the room.

Patrick hesitated, still gripping the chains before he shoved me back. I hissed in pain as my shoulders touched the silver, grimacing.

Laurent stood at the entrance as the door shut firmly behind him. He wore all black, the EH logo stitched onto his leather jacket. He'd aged since the last time I'd seen him, though that didn't surprise me. He'd been young when he'd killed my mate.

"Leave," Laurent ordered, not even sparing a glance toward his son.

"But—"

Laurent's eyes flicked toward Patrick in warning. His son shot me one last dark look before turning on his heel and disappearing out the door.

And then it was just the two of us. Me... and my mate's murderer.

I had never wanted to kill anyone more than Laurent Argent.

And of course right now, I wasn't able to.

"So." He took a few steps forward, stopping just feet away. "You're not looking too well, Noah."

"Unchain me and we'll see how well I'll be then," I replied coldly.

Laurent said nothing. He stood there, watching me, nothing but icy calculation in his eyes.

"This so-called proof that you have on me about leading a rebellion is a lie, isn't it." I didn't phrase that as a question, the truth sinking into my bones.

"It is." He didn't even try to deny it. "I needed a reason to finally break the rules our predecessors had set."

"The attacks..."

"Are ones we've incited," Laurent says. The edges of his lips twitch. "It was easy enough. Dangle bait in front of a monster long enough and they'll reveal their true colors."

My heart sunk into my stomach thinking about everyone who had been implicated in Laurent's cold and twisted plans. It was beyond ridiculous that someone could be this fucked up instead of accepting what could possibly be a new world.

It took me a while to understand what he was saying. "You purposely set those humans up." All those lives... all of those people who'd gone missing...

"They were nobodies," Laurent shrugged. "Sacrifices made for the good of all."

For the first time since Sydney's betrayal, I felt rage building in my chest. All these years I'd tried to keep my people in order to protect them. I followed their rules. Bowed to them. And now I realized it had all been for nothing. "You're breaking your own laws," I pointed out. "This wasn't part of our agreement. I allowed you to take those who broke your rules, who attacked and killed humans, and you agreed to arrest them and only release them once they were rehabilitated."

He snorted, shaking his head. "Oh, come now, Noah. Don't be so naive. Do you really believe that monsters can change who they are?"

"The centers..."

"Were a lie." He stared me down, waiting for me to realize what he'd meant. "You see, we were only able to kill supernaturals once they'd broken the laws," Laurent continued. "The rehabilitation centers were a cover. Did you really believe we were rehabilitating monsters just to release them back into the wild to kill again?" His laugh lashed through my skull painfully.

"And you call me the monster."

"We did what we must," Laurent spat, showing the first real emotion I've ever seen from him. Fury flashed in his eyes before disappearing just as quickly as it had come. He walked around the chair, hands behind his back. "I never chose this life," he continued. "I was given this role. Trained for it my entire life just as my father had and his father before him. It's not just a job—it's our duty to protect humanity from monsters such as you."

"So killing us off..."

"Is the only real solution," Laurent finished for me. "I quickly realized that, no matter how much we controlled, no matter what rules we put in place, there would always be some who would break them. And you..." He stopped in front of me. "I'd realized breaking you would never be enough. Even after her death, you still had too much power."

"So why didn't you kill me?" I asked with disgust and curiosity.

"Because that would lead to war," Laurent replied, shrugging. "And why would I start a war when I could easily plant evidence that incriminated you? No one would dare voice their opposition if you, I don't know, were planning to overthrow us."

"The perfect excuse." My mind finally connected all the dots.

Laurent had been baiting the supernaturals, making it seem as if there was something larger at play that Elite Humanity would have to take down. He'd given his people an excuse to finally wipe us all out—to get rid of the problem entirely. And I hadn't realized it. Hadn't stopped it in time.

I'd failed.

Instead of feeling defeated, all I felt was rage. I jolted forward, fighting the chains even as they burned into my skin. My canines extended, flashing as I snarled. "When I get out of here..."

"Oh, but you aren't," Laurent replied, straightening the lapel of his jacket. "Even if you were to break out of those chains, which I'm sure you can't, you wouldn't be able to kill me."

"And why's that?" I growled.

"Because then she would die as well... just like your mate."

His words stopped me cold. "Sydney."

"See." He wagged a finger toward me, "I know how you feel about her. And that was your mistake. You gave me a weakness to exploit."

"You'd kill your own daughter?" It didn't surprise me. I'd known Laurent for years. I'd watched as he murdered my mate, an innocent woman, just to keep me in line. He would do anything to keep the power he'd always wanted. To get back at us for his wife's betrayal.

Darkness shadowed his face. "She's no daughter of mine," he spat. "Not if she's sleeping with creatures such as you." There was venom in his voice, a hatred so dark and dangerous.

I knew what had happened to his wife. She'd fallen in love with a Werewolf. Ran away with him. I also knew what he'd done to her. Laurent had tracked them down with his eldest son and daughter, forcing them to watch as he killed, first the Werewolf, then their mother. From what I'd heard, he hadn't been merciful. Instead, he'd cut her to ribbons, slicing her skin until it had peeled from her bones.

Fear shot down my spine, my beast anxiously whining at the thought of Laurent hurting Sydney. Despite the betrayal, despite what she was, I still couldn't deny the way I felt about her. She was my second chance. The mate I never thought I could have again. The one I might never have.

"If you hurt her..." I pulled at the chains again, desperately wishing I could sink my fangs into his neck, shredding the life from his body.

Laurent clicked his tongue like a disappointing father. "I don't think you're in any position to be making threats." He started for the door, only hesitating as he reached for the handle. "You will give us a confession that you were leading a rebellion against Elite Humanity. If you do not, Sydney will be the one to face the consequences. And so will everyone else you love."

And then he was gone.

DEATH TO THOSE WE LOVE

Lawson made calls as we headed toward Elite Humanity headquarters. They were stationed outside of New York to avoid breaking the laws they'd set for sanctuary cities. Something I was surprised to find that Lawson wasn't informed about. In fact, he had said that as far as they aware EH headquarters was in another state. For hours he drove while I sat in the passenger seat, nervously chewing at my thumbnail or simply staring out the window. It seemed as if we were going too slow, taking too much time. Time that could mean Noah was being tortured.

If he was even still alive. *God, please be alive.*

Lawson hung up the phone, tossing it into the cup holder between us once more. He had done this a few times while we had been driving and every time I became more curious as to who he was speaking with. The anger in his voice constantly showed how frustrated he was.

"Who did you call?" I asked, finally deciding to converse with him and distract myself.

"Reinforcements."

Reinforcements... we will definitely need those. "How many?"

His face darkened, hands tightening on the wheel, showing the aggravation at my questions that registered loud and clear. "All of them."

I didn't know who he called, but I assumed it was the rest of his people. Possibly more than that. If Noah was a king, it wouldn't surprise me that he had allies. I just hoped they would be enough.

"What's the plan?" I asked hesitantly, hoping he would tell me anything.

"They'll meet us there. The first wave will cause a distraction, attacking headquarters straight on. You and I will sneak in through the chaos to find my brother," Lawson explained. He made it sound like he was used to this. Like he did this more than once. "I'll need to know the exact layout."

I told him everything, from the exits to the possible places my father might be keeping Noah. Most likely, he'd have him in one of the interrogation cells. They were made of cement and iron, and laced with silver to weaken almost any supernatural. The only issue was that those cells were deep underground, and we had about a thousand Elite Humanity agents to get through.

"You'll want to stop the car about a mile out," I told him. "EH has cameras everywhere, but I know a spot where we can sneak in. There's an old emergency tunnel that hasn't been used in years. It was built just in case they were ever under attack." I paused. "Which, now I guess they are."

Lawson nodded, stepping on the gas. We took the back roads, with me giving directions every now and then. Elite Humanity's headquarters were in the heart of the woods, far away from the closest towns. They'd done that on purpose, taking advantage of the acres surrounding the building to train agents. When we finally neared the place, I pointed to the side of the road.

"There."

He pulled over, cutting the engine before checking his phone. "The others are almost in place. Are the cameras still working in the old tunnel?"

"I'm not sure," I glanced out the window, trying to find the entrance through the trees. I knew these woods inside and out, and I'd used the emergency tunnel more than once to sneak out every now and then. "There shouldn't be. I've used it a few times and my father had never said anything about it to me."

Lawson looked uncertain, but didn't argue. He kept his eyes on his phone, waiting for the notification his reinforcements were ready. I sat there nervously, barely able to contain my desperation. All I wanted to do was storm in there and get Noah out. Waiting was slowly killing me, and the thought of what I might find... hurt me even more.

Finally, Lawson's screen lit up, causing my heart to lurch as he read the text. "They're in place."

Hopping out of the car, I took the lead. My boots crunched on small rocks that lined the road as I made my way onto the grass and headed toward the treeline. It was difficult to maneuver through the wild underbrush while I kept an eye out for the entrance, but I knew it was around here somewhere...

"There," I replied. The steel door, half hidden behind some bushes, as if it hadn't been touched in years. I would have to put my ID number in to get into the building, and there was a good chance that when I did, it would alert my father. However, I didn't bother to tell Lawson that because there was also a 50% chance no one would catch my entry.

A risk I was willing to take for Noah.

Moving the brush from the side of the entrance, I located the silver metal keypad. Nerves began to flutter my stomach as I took a deep breath, quickly typing in my ID number, waiting for the light to turn from red to green. As the seconds ticked by, I felt like I was going to explode, but then with a stroke of luck the green light glowed and the sound of the lock clicking brought me reassurance we're one step closer to Noah.

When we stepped into the tunnel, the door shut behind us and everything went dark. "Don't move... I'll get the light on my phone."

Laughter escaped Lawson's mouth at my words. "You better hurry because you're going to need it. I, on the other hand, don't."

Grabbing my phone, I groaned inwardly at his comment as I turned the flashlight on, watching as the soft glow lit up the small portion of the tunnel in front of me. The tunnel was deathly silent, a chill creeping in from beyond the shadows. Our footsteps echoed as we headed down beneath the ground, deeper into danger but closer to Noah. I knew this would lead straight to the back corridors, where EH used most of the rooms for storage. The cells would be a floor or two down, depending on where they put him.

In the end, all of it was hope. Hope we didn't get caught and hope he was still alive.

"Are you sure your distraction will work?" I whispered, after what felt like an eternity of silence between us.

"It'll work," Lawson replied firmly.

Not that we would know. We were taking the back way in. His plan had his pack at the front of the buildings, pulling the agents toward that direction while we snuck in. I'm not sure how well it would work, but I guess we were about to find out.

The corridor led to another door, forcing me to enter my code once again. Slipping through, I paused as I assessed which direction to go. The corridor split in two. The left I knew led toward the upper levels of the building—a place we actively wanted to avoid. The right would lead down into the basement and the cells. Just as I was about to turn right, everything went dark. Red lights flickered on, the sounds of a warning siren echoing down the hall. Sounds of gunshots and screams filtered through the hallway from the left.

"That would be the reinforcements," Lawson said quietly.

I tried not to think about what was happening above us. Taking the right, I started toward the stairs, taking them two at a time to the level just below us. I didn't think there would be any agents down here now that the alarm had gone off.

But I was wrong.

"Hey!" Two agents jolted as I turned the corner, drawing their guns. Two shots rang, hitting the cement wall beside me as I ducked back around the corner.

"Crap," I muttered, glancing back at Lawson.

He snarled. "Silver bullets?"

"Most likely."

"Bring it on." His claws snapped out, canines elongating as he growled. "I'll distract them. You find my brother." Before I could stop him, he darted around the corner.

There was a sharp scream before it was abruptly cut off. Another shot rang out. I didn't want to leave him behind, but I knew we were running out of time. His reinforcements would only distract Elite Humanity for so long, and I needed to get Noah out of there before then.

Sprinting across the opening, I continued down the hallway toward the first set of cells. Doors lined the corridor, the red light making it all look like a set out of a thriller movie as screams of agony and gunfire echoed in the distance. Time wasn't on my side, and pressing forward, I desperately scouted to find out which room Noah was in.

The first cell was empty. As was the next, and the next. I felt like everything was falling apart with every room I searched, but as I raced toward one of the last doors, fate found another path for me.

"Noah..." I gasped the moment I opened the door, my eyes setting upon his bulky frame.

He sat in a silver-plated chair, hunched over. Pain was etched into every line on his face. Burn marks scattered along his chest, tiny holes burnt around the edges and crusted with crimson. The entire room reeked of burnt flesh and blood.

For a moment, I stood there frozen, my eyes raking down his body. The breath fled from my lungs, his pain becoming mine. It took him a few seconds to realize he wasn't alone as he struggled to raise his head, a look of defeat upon his face as his eyes met mine.

Recognition flickered in his eyes before it was replaced with something else. Something darker. A hunger and hatred that broke my heart in two.

"What are you doing here," he snarled.

"Noah..." I took one step into the room and stopped.

"Get out." His words were bitingly cold. "Leave."

"No." We didn't have time for this. Any minute, Elite Humanity agents might descend on us. I didn't know how much longer Lawson could hold them off.

I hurried toward the chair, slipping my pin from my pocket. The chains were all connected and locked into place. It was easy enough to pick—I'd been doing that since I could hold a lock pick. As the silver fell from his body, he lunged. Gripping me by the throat, Noah snarled, teeth flashing inches from my face.

"You betrayed me," he snarled, pushing me until my back hit the door.

"I'm sorry," I whispered, tears pricking my eyes. "I didn't mean to. I didn't mean for any of this to happen."

I could see the internal struggle on his face. I knew he hated me for what I did, for what I was. But I could also see the truth.

"Please, Noah," I begged. "Please believe me."

"And why should I?" He shook his head, fighting off whatever argument he was having with himself. "You're one of them."

"I'm not," I swore. "Maybe before. But not now."

He hesitated, his eyes locking with mine. "And what changed?"

Slowly, I took his hand in mine, pulling him closer. My head tilted back, lips begging to reach his. "I fell in love with you," I whispered.

Breath hissed from his lips before they claimed mine. Fire ripped through me, erasing any and all worries. My fingers raked through his hair, drawing him closer. All I wanted was to feel him against me, safe and...

"Isn't that romantic."

We broke apart, whipping around to face my brother. Patrick stood in the doorway, gun aimed at me. Blood splattered across his cheeks, his hands coated in it. I didn't want to think about whose blood it was, but I had no doubt that a lot of those reinforcements wouldn't be going home today. Noah growled, stepping between us as he shielded my body with his own.

"Move, mutt," Patrick hissed. "You'll die soon enough."

"No." Noah refused to budge. Despite how weak he was, he stood his ground.

"Patrick, please," I begged, though I knew it was useless. "Just let us go."

"Let you go?" Patrick laughed, a bitter sound. "No, I don't think so. You don't just get to walk out of here after betraying us."

Noah glanced at me, confused.

"Oh, she didn't tell you about her little friends upstairs?" Patrick's lip curled. "Elite Humanity is under attack. And I know it was you. I saw you come in through the emergency tunnel with this mutt's brother. Too bad he didn't die when he was supposed to." Noah growled in warning. "You betrayed your own people," Patrick continued, unfazed. "Father will reward me for executing the traitor and her dog pet."

I saw the moment he pulled the trigger. My eyes shut just as the gunshot rang out. There was a gurgled sound, a thud, then nothing at all. Opening my eyes, I found Patrick sprawled on the floor, his neck twisted at an odd angle. His empty eyes stared up at me, mouth parted in surprise.

"Finally," Lawson drawled, wiping his hands on his bloodied shirt. "I'm surprised that the kid managed to live as long as he did."

I could do nothing but stare at the body of my brother. I knew I was supposed to feel something—anything. He was my brother, after all.

But I didn't. If I had to feel anything, it would have been relief.

FOREVER & ALWAYS

SYDNEY

"We need to go." Noah took my hand, hauling me toward the door. Still in shock, trying to process what the hell had just happened, I nodded before numbly following him. My brother was my father's favorite, and Noah was right to hurry us to get out of there. I could only imagine what hell my father would rain down upon everyone to get vengeance for my brother's death.

Moving down the hallway, Lawson trailed after us as we raced through the darkness back the way we had come. However, as we reached a split, they stopped.

"Sydney, which way?" Noah asked. When I didn't respond, he forced me to face him. "Which way?" he repeated slowly, softer this time.

"Right," I mumbled.

The rest was a haze as he stumbled through the half-lit halls, the flashing warning lights painting everything red. We passed two bodies, their throats ripped open. Lawson's doing, I assumed, though I didn't really register it. It seemed like an eternity before we finally were back in the emergency tunnel, heading up toward the forest.

The smell of fresh air, becoming clearer.

As soon as we were outside, I felt the weight of what I'd just done. I'd helped supernaturals break into headquarters, allowing them to attack my own people. It was because of me that Lawson killed my brother. My father would never forgive me for this.

He would never let this go unpunished.

"Car?" Noah asked, glancing toward Lawson.

"Just up ahead." Lawson took the lead, stalking through the underbrush.

Tears pricked my eyes as I followed, trailing behind them. The moment we reached the car Lawson hopped behind the wheel as Noah climbed into the front, leaving the backseat to me. I honestly didn't mind it though, because the moment Lawson peeled out going back the way he came all I could was curl up on myself trying to accept everything that had just happened.

The entire drive back to Noah's house seemed like a blur. Noah's voice was soft as he made a few calls, his eyes darting back to me in the back seat more than once. But I was too tired to reassure him that I was fine.

Because I wasn't.

I'd just given up everything I knew for him. And, while I didn't regret my choice, I knew we would have to deal with the consequences later. Consequences that wouldn't easily be averted. As Lawson pulled through the steel gates of Noah's home, he stopped just before the front steps before cutting the engine. I slipped out of the back seat, noticing Noah's grimace as he shut the door behind him. The bullet wound in his chest, along with all the others, still hadn't healed.

And they wouldn't, not with the silver bullet still in there.

Walking to his side, I placed my arm around Noah, letting him lean against me as we headed up the steps of his house. I wasn't sure how safe it was, but it was the only place we could go that would have some sort of protection against my father and his vengeance. Through the trees, I spotted a few men stationed around the property, Werewolves I assumed were part of his security team.

The door quickly opened, the butler waiting for us as his eyes scanned the driveway towards the gate. Obviously he was looking to make sure the coast was clear before his eyes settled upon Noah. Without hesitation, he immediately headed upstairs. Lawson came up the otherside of Noah as he wrapped his arms around his brother, taking his weight from me, as he helped him up the stairs.

I wasn't sure what to do, or where my place was in his home. But I trailed behind them quietly as I watched Lawson help Noah to his bed before backing away.

"How much time do you think we have before they retaliate?" Lawson asked as the butler reappeared, hurrying to Noah's side with a first aid kit.

"I'm not sure," Noah replied, glancing at me. As if I was supposed to know the answer to that question. I couldn't even think straight let alone know what my father was probably in the process of doing.

Shrugging my shoulders with a heavy sigh, my chest aching over what had happened. I took a moment to try and think it all through. "Whatever your friends did might give us enough time to recoup. The attack might have drawn too much attention to Elite Humanity and they wouldn't want normal humans to know about all of this. But my father will be out for revenge. I'm sure of that. Especially with Patrick—" The words died in my throat.

Noah's eyes flicked toward Lawson with concern, knowing full well what I was getting at. "You'll need to lie low for a bit. Maybe get out of the city."

"I'm not going anywhere," Lawson argued.

"Yes, you are." There was power behind Noah's words, a power Lawson clearly couldn't disobey. I watched as Lawson's eyes lowered while he gritted his teeth. It was clear he wanted to fight against the request, but he knew he couldn't. He would have to obey what his brother was saying.

"I can head out west. But I won't be gone for long," he warned. "You can't order me away forever."

"Grab a bag and go," Noah told him. "Call me when you're safe."

"And you?" Lawson looked between me and Noah. "What will you do?"

"I'll deal with it. Just get out of here before EH comes after you." Noah grimaced as his butler addressed his wounds, it was clear it was painful but as I processed their conversation I knew that whatever they were planning wouldn't work.

"No—wait, you can't."

Lawson and Noah both looked at me with confusion as they furrowed their brows. "What do you mean can't? My brother has to leave Sydney."

"No, I know that," I replied, running my hand through my hair as I tried to think quickly. "You can't go somewhere that's going to be obvious. Nowhere with connections because that's exactly what's going to get you caught."

"Look, I have been doing this a lot longer than you girl—"

"Lawson, enough," Noah snapped as he grimaced again. His words laced with venom over the way Lawson had spoken to me. "Sydney, what are you talking about?"

My father wasn't a stupid man by far, and if Lawson was trying to go west right now because he knew someone... well, it meant my father knew too. There wasn't a thing that man didn't know which would only put Lawson in danger.

"My father knows everything about you, Lawson. You can't do what you usually do, and you can't use anything that is able to be tracked. They will just find you."

Lawson hesitated, his eyes glancing towards Noah at my words. "What do you want me to do then?"

Before Noah could even reply, I opened my mouth wanting to provide a solution. "I have somewhere you can go. He won't find you."

Both Noah and Lawson seemed hesitant at my outburst, but I couldn't help myself. Regardless of what happened to my brother and my entire life being turned upside down, I wanted to help them. I wanted to help Noah, because after everything that I had done to them...

I felt like I owed them. I did owe them.

"Okay," Noah sighed, nodding his head. "What do you have in mind?"

There was a twinkle of pride in his eyes that made the frown upon my face turn up into a small smile that warmed my heart. "My mother kept journals of a place she used to visit with Toran, the shifter she loved. It's an island down in Georgia. My father would never expect you to go there, Lawson. Hell, he probably doesn't even know I have my mothers journals."

Lawson didn't trust me, that much was evident. However, after everything I had done I wanted to earn his respect, with a sigh of acceptance, he nodded. "Write the information down for me. I'll leave within the hour."

Noah only nodded as he watched his brother slip out the door. Silence consumed the room as my eyes turned from the door towards Noah. I hated this, hated how things turned out.

"I've got it from here, James," Noah finally said to the butler as he gently took the bandages from James, motioning toward the door. James' eyes glanced from his master to me before he nodded.

"I'll be downstairs if you need me," James replied, bowing his head slightly.

As soon as he was gone, Noah's gaze turned toward me. "Did you know?"

"Know what?" I asked with confusion as I stepped closer towards him.

"That your father was the one behind the attacks."

Standing before him in complete confusion, I shook my head. "What?"

Noah grimaced as he tried to wrap the bandages around his waist. My instincts swiftly kicked in as I sat beside him on the bed, taking the bandages from him while he rested.

"Laurent admitted everything to me," Noah said quietly. "He used people as bait, needing an excuse to finally wipe us all out for good."

My hands froze as heartache filled me. I had known my father's hatred for the creatures only grew stronger after what my mother did to him, but I had no idea that he would stoop to the levels he had taken. "No, I didn't know about that."

Covering his hand with mine, Noah used his other hand to lift my chin so I was forced to meet his gaze. "Did you mean what you said back there?"

I knew what he was referring to and closing my eyes I nuzzled the side of my face into his hand with a smile on my lips. "Every word, Noah. I love you."

An emotion I couldn't identify flickered in his eyes. I didn't have much time to think about it as he pulled me toward him. Electricity sparked along my spine as our lips crashed together. I could feel his hunger, his desire.

I'd never felt love like this. Yet, I had yearned for it my entire life. Trying to hold back the tears that threatened to fall over the realization of the pain I had caused him, I relished in the soft and tender moment with him. His thumb brushing along my cheek, followed by his lips as he kissed them away.

"Noah," I whimpered, "please forgive me."

A soft chuckle left his lips as I looked once more up into his eyes. "I've already forgiven you," he replied, claiming me once more.

His words were a fire that licked at the wounds of my heart. Pulling me on top of him, a hiss of pain escaped his lips as my thighs settled on either side of his waist. My hands gently ran along his chest, feeling the damage my family had done to him.

No matter the pain he was feeling, it didn't stop him from wanting me. His hand slowly slipped between us, running along the inside of my thigh before finding my center. I couldn't help myself, my hips ground against his fingers. The feeling of him against me filled the emptiness inside. And I craved more.

I craved all of him, and I always would.

Helping him as he tried to remove my shirt, I pulled it over my head, claiming his lips once more as I reveled in the feeling of his hands gliding along my waist. One by one, things slowly fell into place. My bra dropped to the floor. His claws rippled at the fabric of my leggings as he tore through them and the black satin panties I had underneath.

Slow tantalizing kisses were left along my neck by him as he trailed down over my collar bone down towards my left breast, his tongue swirling around my exposed nipple as I gasped in pleasure. The feeling of his teeth gently toying with it, the mixture of pain and pleasure sending chills across my skin, raised the hairs along the back of my neck.

"All I want is you," I whispered, as I lifted his chin to steal another kiss. "I don't care if the whole world is after us. As long as I have you, I can face anything."

It was all he needed to hear as he flipped me to the side, my back pressed against his chest. The feeling of his cock against my entrance, already wet and waiting for him. He thrusted deep inside me, filling and stretching me so completely, without mercy. His hand gripped my hip, keeping me in place as the force of his thrusts nearly sent me over the edge. His other hand slipped beneath my waist as his thumb rubbed circles around my clit relentlessly.

And God, did he fuck me like it was the last thing he'd ever do. I took it all, biting into the pillow with muted screams as I writhed in his arms. I took all of him, over and over, until I thought he might break me.

"Make me yours," I whispered.

I knew I was his second chance mate. I had only read about it in stories, and knew how rare it was for Lycans to have such a thing—which was probably why my father killed Roya and didn't bat an eye at the possibility of Noah having another mate.

"If I do that... you know what that means right?" Noah murmured, his lips brushing against his ear.

I did know what it meant. It meant I would forever be his, my soul linked to his own—to live an eternity at his side. "Yes, I do. An forever with you seems like the perfect adventure."

I felt his teeth sink into my shoulder at my words, a cry escaping my lips before the pain turned into absolutely pleasure. A high that topped any type of drug that could have possibly been out there. I wanted all of it, all of him. The moment I felt the high slowly start to slip his thumb pinched my clit, sending sparks of pleasure across me once more as he finished marking me for all eternity. I was barely sane, my thoughts incoherent. All I could feel was his body pressed against mine, his cock deep inside me, and I've never wanted a moment to last forever like I did just then.

His body tensed as his lips pulled away, the heat of my blood in his mouth from my shoulder lingering. Noah groaned, thrusting deep inside me again. Shivers rolled down my spine, the most intense orgasm I'd ever had ravaging my body. We had come together, our souls now intertwined—forever.

Wrapping his arms around me, he pulled me close to him, bringing his lips to my shoulder. The last kiss was long as if he never wanted this to end.

"You're mine now," he said softly, kissing the mark he'd left behind on my skin. "You're mine, Sydney. Now and forever."

His words were the truest thing I had ever heard, and even with war approaching, my father at the ready, I knew I'd follow this man till my last breath left my body.

I loved him, and I would for the rest of my life.

Also By